HARPER'S WEEKLY.
A JOURNAL OF CIVILIZATION.

Vol. VI.—No. 299.] NEW YORK, SATURDAY, SEPTEMBER 20, 1862. [SINGLE COPIES SIX CENTS. $2 50 PER YEAR IN ADVANCE.

Entered according to Act of Congress, in the Year 1862, by Harper & Brothers, in the Clerk's Office of the District Court for the Southern District of New York.

A GALLANT COLOR-BEARER.—[See Next Page.]

Duane Finch: The Civil War and the Uncivil West

Stuart L. Scott

Moscow, Idaho
2024

Duane Finch:
The Civil War and the Uncivil West

Stuart L. Scott

Published by
Stuart L. Scott
112 S. Main St.
Moscow, Idaho

Copyright Stuart L. Scott, 2024

ISBN print: 978-1-7375429-3-3

Printed by Ingram/Spark

Cover Design by: Tania Suarez Mendoza
Cover Image from Harper's Weekly, Saturday, Sept 20, 1862

This is a work of fiction. Many of the characters were inspired by historical research and the reminiscences of the main character. However, the events are fictionalized and do not represent actions attributable to any specific person living or dead.

Dedications:

To Ray Majeski, a friend for life. Always a giver and never a taker. And to Jerry O'Donnell, a friend who has now passed on. Jerry was the man whose simple framing of a thought encouraged me to get into therapy. "Stu, do you know any doctor who would try to remove his own appendix?"

Contents

Introduction

As I started researching this new story, I began with the events that will play out in the story arc, and I often found some long-cherished family stories weren't true. My Great-Great Grandfather Duane Finch was not the Pony Express Station Agent at Trinidad, Colorado. Nor was he a personal friend of Kit Carson. He did not donate the land for Kit Carson Park in Trinidad. Ouch! These family mythologies are untrue, and none of them will appear in my tale. But that does not mean his story isn't a great historical adventure.

He served during the Civil War. Among his battles were Shiloh, Corinth, Jackson, Vicksburg, and Atlanta. Wounded and captured, he was confined in the infamous Andersonville prison camp. Next, he was the Barlow and Sanderson Stage Company agent at Trinidad and chose the original stage route over Raton Pass to Santa Fe. Finally, he had a long career in public service: postmaster, county sheriff, City Treasurer and Police Court Magistrate Judge.

Stuart Scott.

"The only thing necessary for evil to triumph in the world is that good men do nothing."

Edmund Burke

Prologue

1930

My father, James Finch, gave all his boys names with double initials. Here I am Duane Devee. My brother Burns Brannon lived over in Severty, Kansas. My brother Clement Cassius, and my sister Nelda, are in West Union, Iowa. Nelda got spared Dad's double letter system, with a middle name of Hanna. But she did marry a Nelson: double letters again. So, I'm still considering if I'm supposed to keep Dad's naming tradition alive? Will my first son be Alonzo Abraham/ Or Ezekial Ebenezer?

My Dad managed the budget for our town. West Union is the biggest town in Fayette County, Iowa, with ten thousand folks calling it home. Burns has passed, but his family remains in Severty, Kansas. Clem kept a dry goods store here in West Union. But he has passed on now, too.

In 1854, Dad was hired by a group of men from Dubuque and points farther east to help with their planned construction of rail connects through Fayette county. The company was to be called the Mississippi and Missouri Railroad Company.

Dad kept a corner of our parlor as his own private office area. Two easels did the job. Sheets of paper showed the intended routes of the major east-west lines.

In 1858, one easel displayed the Mississippi and Missouri Railroad spur lines. The other easel featured a large copy of the Henry Poor railroad map. The Poor map showed and named all the rail lines that traversed the country from the east coast out through Nebraska, Kansas, and Texas. These lines marked the new iron rivers for commerce that might unchain us from the limits of our geography.

1. So It Begins

West Union, Iowa 1861

In July 1860, with my 18th birthday, I became old enough to join the Masonic Lodge. I wanted to be a "traveling man," like my father and grandfather before him. These were men who believed in brotherly love, truth, respect for women and always operating, in all dealings, 'on the level.'

In August 1860, I took the obligation of the first degree leading to becoming a "Master Mason." I had Dad's help memorizing the obligation that I'd need to recite in open lodge. In December, I knelt and received the second Masonic degree.

In March 1861, I knelt for the third time at the masonic altar and was raised to the third degree of "Master Mason." I was instructed in certain masonic means of recognition and means of requesting masonic help and charity, one brother Mason to another.

* * *

It was April 25, 1861, just two weeks after the Confederates attacked Fort Sumter, when I signed up to fight for the Union. So did five of my long-time friends from a combination of church, school, and work. Amos Holt and Bill Wenger were friends from our church. They both worked in the same dry goods mercantile as I did. The Evans brothers, Jonathan and David, also would raise their hands along with me. Our families attended different Methodist Churches; the Evans brothers were Evangelical Methodists, while we were not.

The sixth, Dan Daniels, was the oldest among us at twenty-five and the only married man. He was our reader and thinker. His job as the town librarian suited him well. I had to ask. "How come you are volunteering and leaving your wife behind?"

"I'll tell you, Duane, this thing that's about to start is going to keep growing until the whole country is involved. It is not going to be good, or pretty, or heroic, just bloody." I listened, but didn't yet understand what Dan saw on the horizon.

So I asked, "You think so. Why?"

"Well, you know about the attack on Fort Sumter at Charleston?"

I nodded a silent yes.

"See, all the extra time there in the library, I get to read the newspapers that come in. Here's the deal, according to the New York papers. The Governor of South Carolina demanded that President Lincoln surrender the fort, or they would begin bombarding it in 24 hours. Do you know what Lincoln did?"

I didn't and told him so.

"The President told the governor that he would withdraw the garrison that very day, and not return to South Carolina, if the state would not attack." Dan paused, letting me take in the full measure of Lincoln's offer. "And they attacked anyway. They chose to start this war." Again, the librarian paused, moving his gaze from my face to somewhere above my head, at some unknown shape off in the distant depths of the sky.

"Duane, I don't believe we could or should shrink from the coming fight."

Then he faced me again. "Do you know who Thomas Paine was?"

I remembered the name from school, but nothing about the man.

"Paine said about our Revolutionary War, 'If there must be trouble, let it be in my day, that my child may have peace.' God bless the Union and God bless President Lincoln. I'm going now."

Then he grabbed me by my shoulders and spoke full on to my face. "But I'm glad not to be going alone." No words came to me, so I clasped my arm to his back, and we turned, shoulder to shoulder now, and joined our companions, who waited outside the Sheriff's Office.

Inside, Sheriff Gott McPherson was expecting our arrival. His mustache and trimmed beard served to partially conceal a collection of scars that collectively spoke volumes about the past encounters of their 60ish owner. He rose from behind his desk and pointed to a table farther back towards the visible bars of two cells. An American flag lay across the tabletop. "Come over here boys and place your right hand upon our flag."

And we did. The room was silent; the background sounds of the larger world faded to the depths of my consciousness as Sheriff McPherson spoke, his every word softly tinged with the trill of his native Scottish burr. "I canna enlist you into the army, so I'm swearing you as my special deputies to serve from now until you reach Fort Madison and muster in." His eyes moved across our line of faces, looking for any dissent. Seeing none, he took up a small leather-bound book from his desktop and began to read.

"For, as long as but a hundred of us remain alive, never will we on any condition be brought under the rule of godless slavers. It is

4

in truth not for glory, nor for riches, nor honor that we fight, but for freedom and our blessed Union. For this alone, which no honest man gives up but with life itself.”

He paused and returned the still-open book to the desk. Clearing his throat, he spoke again. “Raise your right hands now.”

Six hands shot up.

“Do you swear by Almighty God and your sacred honor to defend the constitution and the Union, and follow the orders of the officers appointed to lead you?”

Then came a moment of silence. I didn’t know if the McPherson oath ceremony was completed, so I cut quick sideways glances at my friends. We all nodded in agreement, faced front and, as one, voiced a hearty “Yes.”

Sheriff McPherson came around his desk and shook our hands. Reaching inside his coat, he distributed a fist full of cigars. Smoker or non-smoker didn’t matter at the moment. The sheriff then took a wooden match from a box on his desk and struck the red fulminate tip on the desktop. The match flared to life, and he lit his own cigar before offering the flame to Dan, who stood nearest him. Only Dan and I chose to light our smokes, with the other four pocketing theirs.

“Fellas, I have one more thing for each of you.” He retrieved six envelopes from his desktop and handed one to each of us. “Keep the letter with you on your way to Fort Madison.”

Inside, we each found a letter on the Sheriff’s Department county stationery. It named us as recent volunteers for the Union army and special deputies for the Fayette County Sheriff’s Department. The letter asked any and all citizens to extend to us every courtesy and kindness as we were traveling on official business to Fort Madison. It was signed by the Sheriff and the Mayor of West Union. The tri-folded letter also held a twenty-dollar bank note.

It was David who voiced the same question that crossed my mind. “Sheriff, what was it you read from the book?”

McPherson smiled and stepped over to the well-used wooden desk. He knocked ash off the tip of his cigar and picked up the small leather-bound book. His lips began to part as a first intended word was almost given voice but stopped. He put down the book, dropped his head, and opened a bottom desk drawer.

First, he retrieved a glass and extracted a bottle of amber liquid, the paper label unreadable from our vantage point. We watched him fill the glass to his satisfaction. Lowering the glass, he used his free hand as a guide to judge the fill level. Satisfied he'd poured enough, the sheriff set down the bottle and took up the glass. He lifted the book from his desktop and stared silently at the page before returning his gaze to the six of us.

"Lads, ma book is a family history I brought from Scotland when I came over, first to Canada and finally to West Union. What I read was part of the Declaration of Arbroath. About 500 years ago, we Scots were fighting for our freedom from the English. The English King, Edward, was a mean bastard and wanted, nay, tried to kill us all. Our heroes, William Wallace and others, gave Edward their declaration. We'd die on our feet rather than live on our knees."

All six of us stood silent, our tongues tied by McPherson's words. The sheriff now returned the book to the desktop. He took a long pull from the amber liquid in his glass, then passed it into the hand of Amos Holt. No explanation or instruction was needed as the glass was passed among us until it was fully drained.

Finally, McPherson broke the silence. "I've told the garrison command you are enroute and you're due to arrive at Fort Madison over at Keokuk on the Mississippi River. It's 180 miles all told, so you have five days to report."

* * *

By silent acclamation, Dan Daniels seemed an agreeable leader to us all. He pointed us up the block towards the Overland Stage Depot. "Come, guys. Let's find out which stage we need and when it passes through." And off we turned and walked down Vine Street under the bright sun.

The warmth of the late April morning brought out the smell of flowers blooming in the yards we passed as we walked down Vine Street. These fragrances masked the ever-present tang of newly deposited horseshit that littered the brick-paved street until its daily removal.

The stage stop was at the corner of Vine and Elm Street, where the business district met the East/West road out of town. Two blackboards displayed chalked arrival and departure times.

"I'll go in and check with the station agent about the best way for us to get to Keokuk, okay?" Dan did a quick visual check for consent from our little group and went inside. Five minutes later, he rejoined us, where everyone was leaning against the wall or sitting on the raised sidewalk.

"Okay, the agent, Mr. Stewart, suggests we take the stage east to Marquette on the Mississippi. Then we book passage on a steamboat and ride downriver towards Keokuk. I know that Fort Madison is just a few miles upriver from there. The depot manager thinks that if we tell the steamboat captain where we're going, he just might make an unscheduled stop to let us off. The stage trip takes a full day. When we get on the river, the boat would have us there in two days.

"Questions?" None appearing, we agreed to go our separate ways. Each of us would make what preparations were needed and say our many goodbyes. As the traffic of people, carts and animals moved by in their own daily rhythms, we agreed to meet back here at the stage depot the next morning for the 8 AM stage.

At eight the next morning, we started our journey; round trip or one way, we knew not: dreamers all.

2.   Mustering In

Keokuk Iowa, June, 1861

Our initial enlistments were for 90 days. I guess Ole Abe figured that was all the time our boys would need to bring the rebels to heel.

June 10, 1861
Dear Folks,

My five friends and I are now members of Company F, of the 3rd Iowa Infantry Regiment. Our company commander is Major C.A. Newcomb. The regiment is commanded by Col. Nelson Williams. Our few actual army sergeants and officers have set us about learning drills and how to march. Necessary stuff, I'm sure, truly more designed to fill our time and keep us in camp. I was expecting some skills that might help keep us alive. Maybe later, I guess.

We drill and march in the clothes we brought with us. The promised uniforms, guns, everything else pretty much, have not been delivered. Fort Madison is perpetually noisy and clouded in its own dust storm from all the marching feet.

There is great emphasis on keeping us busy. We do have free time in the evenings. I'm making new friends, from Fayette County and a whole lot of other towns. They feed us well: not what we'd call good, but not bad either. My new quarrel with the Rebs is how the price of good cigars has shot up. Believe it or not, a decent smoke costs me a nickel.

I hope you and mom are both well, and my thoughts are often back at home. I'll write when I have some news.

Love, Duane

In the first week of June, our uniforms began to arrive. I can say the uniforms all looked similar, but not the same. A dark blue wool coat, lighter blue pants and a black cap. The shoes were brogan type, all cut straight, with no right or left foot, just clod hoppers. We got belts with a stamped U.S. on the brass buckle. Better than nothing, I suppose.

We began to look like soldiers, now that we had Union blue uniforms to wear. I doubt that there was a good Union rifle anywhere in Keokuk, so we waited. Almost every day a new rumor about rifles surfaced.

Governor Sam Kirkwood began hounding Washington for the promised supplies our Iowa boys needed. But nothing came of it. I'll give it to the old boy. Kirkwood wouldn't give up. So next he sent Grenville Dodge, a civil engineer from Council Bluffs, to plead our case. Mr. Dodge succeeded. For that, the governor appointed him a Colonel of the 4th Iowa Infantry.

Finally, in the last week of June, our quartermaster issued rifles. I was now praying for the forgiveness of all my sins as we would soon be leaving training for who knows what. I was supposed to fight the rebels with an old musket and a bayonet that wouldn't stay hooked under the barrel. If I didn't die from it exploding in my hands, it would be through the goodness of Divine Providence. As I lugged this piece of scrap iron into Missouri with my fellow recruits, my life seemed in equal danger from their muskets and from my own. Indians would only fear these guns if they were trying to shoot them.

Rusty smooth-bore muskets had been refitted to fire with percussion caps. Oh, what sour fruit had Governor Kirkwood's and Grenville Dodge's work born. It looked to us like a Confederate Quartermaster handled the order. There were .58 caliber French or Austrian muskets, .72 caliber Prussian guns and other castoffs. As the guns got distributed, I heard a howl of laughter go up. The only ones of the lot that any of us trusted enough to claim were the Enfields and the few Colt revolvers.

The word, or perhaps just the rumor around camp, was that our unit was about to leave Fort Madison for a posting. That would mean our training, such as it was, was over. We were well drilled and if given a fair chance to face the Rebs in a drill competition, they wouldn't have a chance. Soldierly things like fighting as a unit or setting defenses or an ambush, those skills remained to be taught.

* * *

It took two weeks for Dad's letter to catch up with me. By then we had marched to Hannibal, north of St Louis. A small group of rebels and local sympathizers raided Carthage, just to the south. Our Company quickly split into two platoons of 40 men each. My platoon stayed in Hannibal to do guard duty along the river and scout for rebels. The rest were sent by wagon west to Chillicothe, Missouri, to do the same over there.

Alone at my guard post, I prayed that the rebels would pass us by, as I feared my musket might explode or fail me. I prayed that the triangular blade of my bayonet would not fall off again and stab me in the foot.

We stayed on guard duty until the beginning of August, when our second platoon returned from Chillicothe. The ten companies of our regiment dispersed along the northeastern part of Missouri.

Now our war really began. For the next two months, different units fought brief actions with the rebels. We fought small Confederate units and their local supporters at Hagers Woods, Monroe, Kirksville and Shelbina. Companies C and D fought the biggest battle yet, at Carthage.

Missouri was a contested area. The Confederates needed Missouri in the Confederacy to help secure their access to the Mississippi River. In the minds of many of its own citizens, Missouri was Confederate. For the first time, I saw what our weapons and theirs did to men. So far, we had been lucky.

But our luck began to run out in late September.

3.   Blue Mills Crossing

September, 1861

Outside Chillicothe, Missouri, our days of guarding the rail line, rivers and warehouse were now over. Our scouts had discovered a large group of Missouri state guard troops on the move towards Lexington. Their plan was to get this group of new recruits across the Missouri River to join their Confederate brothers outside of Lexington, Missouri.

Our second in command, Lieutenant Scott, took half of our Iowa 3rd to stop them at the Blue Mills crossing. We'd meet up with the 16th Illinois at Liberty, Missouri and together hoped to prevent the rebs from crossing. That was our plan, but not mother nature's or the Confederates'.

We marched through the night in a constant heavy rain that turned the road to mud. Along with us was a small German artillery unit. Their two six-pound cannons moved only with two extra mules hitched to each cannon's carriage. Our brogans sank a full inch into the brown mud of the road.

As we marched two abreast, our heads down, rain ran off the bills of our kepi caps. My view was seldom more than the wet back marching ahead of me. All my ears perceived was the constant noise of trudging feet and of sucking mud, in and out, fighting the release of every shoe.

They ambushed us, from both sides of the road at once. I had no cover and no direction. Retreat, turn and fire into the brush and rain or advance? I didn't know. No shouted orders came to my ear. And for a moment, I did nothing, but stood and waited for my turn to fall face down in the mud.

Finally, something in my empty head spoke. *Run, run, run.* Forward? Back? Unknown, but I guess I chose right, because I'm still alive. I retreated, running, sometimes stumbling over Union bodies, all the time as the rain fell.

Finally, I found an exit from the gauntlet of Confederate fire. My brothers had established a firing line. We were returning fire down the road at the still unseen enemy. Suddenly, when the clouds parted, it all changed. The rain stopped and for a moment, so too the Confederate fire, but now came their screaming charge up the road, directly at us.

One rebel soldier came on straight for me, yelling like a demon. I wasn't shooting at paper targets anymore. This target would shoot back.

My shot took him in the shoulder. The impact of the ball lifted him into the air. His body turned a full backward somersault, landing him in a crumpled heap. He rose from elbows to knees, then standing, and on he came.

I'd just rammed home my cartridge as I looked up and saw him only feet away. I leveled my musket and fired an unaimed shot that struck him square in the chest. As he died at my feet, all the other noise of battle seemed to fade so his final wheezing breaths were audible. I'd killed my first man. God forgive me. But would I forgive myself?

I heard our sergeant and saw him motioning us back. "Retreat—retreat—retreat." I looked at the surrounding men, and they looked back at me, the same ignorant babes in the same vicious woods. As one, we retreated to the sergeants and back beyond them, until waiting officers halted our route. The rebs had whipped us, like the fabled red-headed stepchild.

The next day, I learned most of the rebs had escaped, but one hundred of us had not. Marching back in failure to retrieve our dead, I kept the bravest face I could, notwithstanding puking and crying at what we'd left on the battlefield. The rebels were smart, tough, and would kill us if they could.

* * *

Surgeon at Work During an Engagement

The battle had ended. Some of us walked, some of us hobbled, but we carried away our wounded. The collective dead, both blue and gray, would be handled by the burial crews that marched on as we walked off.

We'd gone into the fight directly from our march, already tired from days of travel. It didn't matter. Our blanket, ground sheet and pup tent, all neatly rolled, we'd carried into battle on our backs. Tired or not, we fought for our brothers, because they would have done the same for us.

Dan walked beside me. Neither of us spoke. He used his musket as a walking staff, its butt down while he gripped the fore end of the stock. We were both half asleep as we followed Sgt. Lakin's lead. To where? Unknown but of no matter, as long as it was away from the battlefield and a chance to rest loomed ahead.

* * *

"All right my boys, you camp here," announced Sgt. Lakin. "Set up your tents." He gestured with his thumb, back behind where he stood "Cook tent and supply wagon will be set up shortly." Then with added emphasis, "hot food tonight; beef, biscuits and real coffee! Not that studhorse piss we've had on the march for the past two days." A spontaneous cheer erupted from us all.

"Now then, I need some volunteers to dig a latrine trench. Who'll be the first to volunteer?" No hands went up. Over the low chorus of sighs, grunts, and other protests, a single voice sang out his own comment. "Shite!" delivered with a bit of Irish lilt.

Sgt. Lakin had spotted the speaker and continued, his face now lit by a broad smile that flared his mustache up into furry handlebars. "Malloy, my lad, thanks for being the first to volunteer." Malloy's smile collapsed into an open-mouthed gape as he set down his kit and walked toward Lakin, kicking the dirt as he walked.

"I still need two more," pausing momentarily, then with his face in another broad smile, came the final word: "Volunteers." Again no hands went up. Lakin pivoted and pointed to me and to Amos. "You and you."

We set down our bedrolls, haversacks, and cartridge belts. Dan smiled as he reached over and took my musket. I passed him the wooden tompion for the barrel. Quick as I could, I dug a cigar and matches from my sack. Then I fell in behind Malloy. Sgt. Lakin pointed at me as I pocketed my cigar and matches.

"Finch, don't light your smoke until I say you can. We'll be passing the medical tents, and I don't want you to get us blown up by the ether vapors."

I nodded my understanding.

I did smell the sweet odor of the ether anesthetic as we approached. There were still screams from inside the two medical tents. Camp knowledge claimed that ether was slow to work. The press of time, blood loss and waiting men didn't always allow for it to do its job before the sawbones did theirs, liberating men from the vestiges of what had been arms or legs.

We passed the medical tents where a line of stretchers awaited their turn. Two orderlies carried a recent patient out through the fluttering tent flaps. His legs were gone, and freshly bandaged stumps remained. As we walked forward, the orderlies disappeared in the opposite direction.

Twenty yards further on, Sgt. Lakin stopped. He seemed to be considering the spot. I wondered why? *Drainage, prevailing winds, the view?*

"This will do, boys. Three feet deep, a foot wide and forty feet long. I'll be back to check on you in an hour." He turned around, leaving us to our task. From ten feet further on, he gave an over-the-shoulder comment. "And you boys can have the honor of christening your work."

* * *

Finally, Dan and I were back at our tent, our bellies now full of beef, beans, and biscuits. We'd both done what we could to clean ourselves from a bucket of hot water provided to every third tent. With friends both new and old, we talked, sometimes of news from home. Sometimes about news from the battlefronts and what we hoped might come or feared could come.

Scores of campfires shone bright, and I decided to have my final cigar of the night in conjunction with my last latrine visit. A row of small fires marked the way to the slit trench. When my ablutions were complete, I still had half a cigar. As I headed back, perhaps halfway between the trench and medical tent, a wagon sat just off the path. The tail board was down beyond the wagon's tarped contents. I sat there to finish my smoke and looked back to camp.

Our fires dotted the moonlit sky with faint columns of light that rose above a sea of pup tents. No screams pierced the sounds of singing, crackling fires and a hundred smaller noises. Curiosity got the best of me. I turned and with my empty hand, lifted the tarp.

There were white, bloodless hands reaching out, amid the uncounted severed remains of limbs, shredded by shot and shell. Rushing to rise, I slipped and ended up seated on the ground with the back of my head resting on the outer edge of the tailgate.

I turned around to pull the tarp back over the wagon load of human debris. A bloodless finger was pointing at my nose. Did what my eyes saw suggest my own waiting fate? As I stood up, I could swear the finger stayed pointed directly into my face.

15

Then I started to gag, fighting to keep my dinner down. I walked back to my bed, silent. I would not put into anyone else's head the picture stuck in my mind of what was beneath the tarp.

* * *

Wounded men from other companies arrived by wagon. The river gave us access to supplies and a route to evacuate the severely wounded. Our dead came back, sometimes in the same wagons as the wounded. As the injured continued to arrive, the very soil began to take on the sharp iron smell of blood, while the air added the odor of disinfectant. There was rarely quiet, even when our guns lay stilled. Wagons, feet, and wounded all combined into a low background hum that seldom gave way to quiet.

None of our group had as yet been wounded. Sitting all together or in the twos and threes of the long nights watching and waiting for the next shot, we spoke aloud less and less. Whiskey was always available from enterprising locals, and our soldiers were good customers. Some of our ranks found that it eased their pains, both mental and physical.

We learned how "Soldier's Joy," whiskey or beer with morphine added, killed the pains. Sometimes the agony came from the "thousand natural shocks that flesh is heir to." The bodily wear and tear: small cuts left to fester, the blister, the boil, and the bug bite. The mosquito, the chigger, the bedbug, and the louse became our companions.

Sometimes the pain was in our minds. Things we had seen that haunted our dreams. Or things we imagined awaiting us. Whatever the source, the torment was no less real. A common sight was a man in Union blue staggering or passed out with a bottle still in hand or resting empty nearby. Our sergeants drank along with their men. The officers, being more mannerly I guess, confined their drinking to their quarters or quiet groupings. Passing sleeping men, we needed no explanation beyond their looks. They were feeling no pain. And who could blame them?

The Evans boys, Jonathan and David, followed the evangelical wing of our Methodist Church. Neither drank nor smoked. True, they had put Sheriff McPherson's toast to their lips, perhaps to sip, given the importance of the moment. But even then, I knew their shares had discretely passed to Amos Holt and Bill Wenger. Their cigars, pocketed with, "I'll save it for later," had been passed along to Dan Daniels and me.

Having enlisted together, our small group of friends arranged ourselves together in camp. I don't mind saying that the other four of us enjoyed a drink, but we still filled our free time without the escape of alcohol. Dan wrote home faithfully every day. I loved my cigars, and Bill had a checkerboard that saw daily use.

All six of us liked to sing and Jonathan was learning to squeeze out a tune from his concertina. I think our music helped keep up our morale and kept us steady on our purpose. It was not uncommon for other men, hearing us, to filter in behind, perhaps joining our voices or even adding the sounds of their banjos and fiddles.

One particular night, Jonathan had just finished playing a song, probably common to soldiers on both sides of the line; "The Girl I Left Behind Me." From the outer edge of our fire's light, a tall stranger, only recognized as a brother-in-arms, spoke up.

"Fella, I know another verse to that old tune, if you want to hear it?" Everyone around our fire, probably twelve men, all sharing bonds of danger and separation from loved ones, replied as one.

"Sing it out brother," and Jonathan squeezed out the familiar first notes. Da da da---da da-

> "I stuck my nose up a Billy Goat's ass,
> And the stink was enough to blind me.
> I'd do that much for the girl I love.
> The girl I left behind me.

Everybody around the fire clapped, hooted or cheered at the bawdy parody. The music brought us an escape, even if only for a moment.

* * *

One of our common bonds brought from home and family was our faith. Four of us enjoyed a drink, but all of us found connection and comfort in prayer. When we found ourselves together around a campfire, we began with a prayer. In prayer, we renewed our common bonds of faith in God, faith in each other and faith in the Union cause. Which of us led the prayer often changed, in a spontaneous response to feelings that came upon us.

The prayers were known to us all from among our common Methodist prayers. Often repeated, I led us in this:

> "God of Life, for all that illuminates the darkness in our own and other lives, thank you. Creator, Redeemer, Sustainer, enable us to see and share your treasure, guiding and upholding into love and life for all men. Amen."

Our two Evangelical affiliated brothers David and Jonathan both used a prayer that was special to them.

> "God of life, your risen Son has gathered us into the church, nourished us with his body and blood, and poured out upon us your Holy Spirit. Grant that we may receive the blessing of your grace, so that we may love you with all our hearts, and gladly feed your sheep in the name of Christ. Amen."

We sang our favorite hymns from the Methodist Hymnal: *Amazing Grace, How Great Thou Art* and *Here I Am, Lord.* There was comfort there for me, sharing a voice in praise of the Lord, music and the warmth of friends around our fire.

I knew that President Lincoln was a man of faith like me, because he appointed and paid chaplains for the entire Union army. There were bibles for anyone without one. Whenever conditions allowed, there were Sunday services. Our chaplains were mostly some type of Protestant, but when of the Catholic persuasion, they preached the bible and not their own brand of theology or morality.

* * *

Finally, on November 1st, we broke camp and those among us who could travel boarded a river steamer barge and moved south to the Benton Barracks at St. Louis. There we stayed through the end of

1861, resting, refitting our weapons, gear, and uniforms. Replacement troops filled out the depletions in our ranks.

Thank the lord, our cast-off muskets were replaced with new .58 caliber Springfields; each musket came with a 17-inch-long socket bayonet. From the brown wood stock to the locking lug that kept my bayonet attached, they were new and for a brief few weeks unmarked.

They also gave out new cartridge pouches for the paper powder tubes and lead Minié slugs. Last in the new issue were pouches for the musket compression caps, and a new haversack for my gear. The new haversack came just in time as the single shoulder strap on my old one was about gone. I was glad to have new gear, but not believing in government generosity, I figured we must be on the verge of something bigger than company-size skirmishes.

I waited quite a while for Dad's latest letter. It had to be repeatedly forwarded along, as it tried to catch up with me. My family and my friends back in West Union were all fine. The rebels had not ventured into Iowa, at least not yet.

My Dad had fought in the Blackhawk War, back in 1832. Having seen what Dad had seen, inaction must have seemed wrong to him. At 50 years old, his only possible service was with the 37th Iowa Volunteer Infantry, known as the Graybeards. All the enlistees were age 45 or older. They would be a 'home guard', supervising crossroads, rail facilities, bridges, and ferry landings. I can't say that I was surprised by his having again answered the call to duty.

Dad was, on the one hand, a kind, friendly, helpful sort of fella. He used to tell me about his time in the militia when he fought Sauk and Fox Indians in Chief Black Hawk's War. In those days, he had been a cold, hard man, none of which showed at home with his family. That was Dad.

Two days after the letter came, a box from the folks arrived. Inside, I found two sets of wool socks and two sets of union suit drawers. Old Abe supplied our uniforms and gear, but we supplied our own underwear and socks. Now at least, after my occasional strip and wash, there was a chance I'd have clean drawers to put on.

I also learned that in September, nineteen men at Upper Iowa University enlisted en masse. Upper Iowa University is a Methodist school eight miles down the road from our town. Some of those who enlisted were faculty and the others students.

After the shellacking the Union army got at Bull Run in July, the need for us all to step up and serve was even more apparent. But enlistments were not keeping up with the Army's needs. The Upper Iowa Union men made a public pledge in the campus chapel. They would go home for one week and act as recruiters among their own friends and neighbors.

And in a week's time, the 19 returned to campus and now numbered 101 men, enough to fill the full complement up to company strength. The entire group was sworn in to the 12th Iowa Volunteer Infantry. Supposedly, the wife of the University President sewed a flag for them. True or not, I liked that.

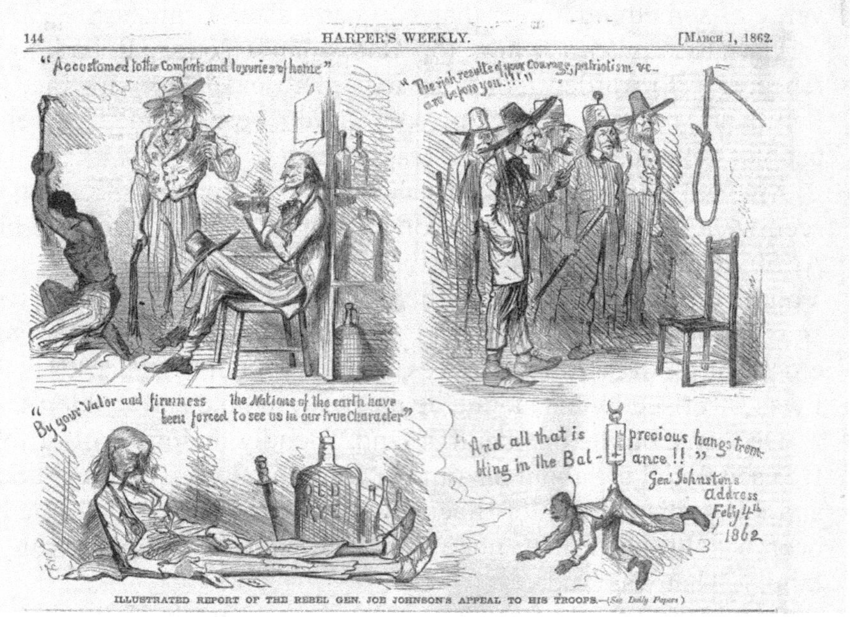

ILLUSTRATED REPORT OF THE REBEL GEN. JOE JOHNSON'S APPEAL TO HIS TROOPS.—(See *Daily Papers*)

I imagine all their hearts beat to the same drum as mine. The Southern slavery of the Negroes was an abomination, an affront to Almighty God.

Harper's Anti-Slavery Cartoons

4.   Railroad Epiphany

St. Louis and Fort Donelson January-April 1862 Dan Daniels was faithful about writing home. His wife's letters back were a good source of information. Our access to real facts was limited, and Ida Daniels' letters gave us insight into the North's strategy.

We were still a young nation, and our rivers were the traditional avenues of both commerce and travel. A new system of rail lines helped move material and men to other places not nestled on our rivers.

The news in Ida Daniels' letters fueled many an evening conversation. Often, she enclosed newspaper clippings. Where the Union had already fought a bloody battle helped us unravel the mystery of what our leaders would attempt to acquire next.

I remembered the two easels that occupied space just left of my dad's desk. He helped build a small part of a developing national system of railroads. When I closed my eyes, I could still picture the Henry Poor Railroad map. I could see the grid of iron lines that amplified our rivers for moving goods and passengers. This was the axis that logically drove our grand strategy.

I filtered the rumors in camp through the news from home. Where were we going? Why go there? I purchased a map when we went into St. Louis on leave. Seeing where battles had been lost or won confirmed my belief.

Our strategic plans centered on three things: rivers, railroads and ports. Common to all three of these places was transportation of goods, be it bullets, beans, or troops.

Victories at Fort Henry on February 5th, along the banks of the Tennessee River, were by a fleet of Union Ironclads and General Grant's Infantry. Then, on February 14th, we forced the rebels out of Fort Donelson on the nearby Cumberland River.

While still at the Benton Barrack outside of St. Louis, I received a letter from my dad. His letter centered on how it had been the 2nd Iowa Infantry who'd won the day at Fort Donelson. A Union Officer, Col. James Tuttle, led the 2nd to victory. Some Confederate troops had managed to make a breakout and headed for the cover of the garrison at Nashville. Still more Confederates, unable to escape, surrendered.

This confirmed that transportation of goods was the key to where we would choose to fight. It seemed clear that Forts Henry and Donelson had been stepping stones in a plan focused on Corinth, Mississippi. There, the Mobile and Ohio Railroad intersected with the Memphis and Charleston Railroad. Corinth seemed to me to be a linchpin of Confederate supply lines.

Finally, we got passes with someplace that was near enough to go: St. Louis, Missouri. St. Louis was the biggest city I'd ever seen. Four of us went together on our eight-hour pass. It was probably good that we did. Dressed in Union blue, our welcome was decidedly mixed. Some people's smiles greeted us. Others turned away, often making comments behind our backs. Missouri sentiments were definitely mixed and strongly held by both sides.

Fortune smiled and I succeeded in replenishing my supply of cigars. I did pass a Masonic lodge hall, as identified by the square and compass emblem painted on the glass of the street door.

Riverside Lodge AF & AM. The time and date of their stated meeting was posted on the door. But all I could do today was keep the information in my memory and hope that fate would allow me to sit in a lodge with my brother Masons sometime in a better future.

Union Troops Capturing Fort Donelson

Our speculation was either cut short or amplified when word came down for us to prepare to depart in two days' time. Those days ended up being filled by our sergeant, making sure that each of us was prepared. Our ammunition pouches carried forty powder wrappers with Minié ball slugs. Did we have our cap pouch full? Blanket rolls, haversacks, mess kits, and canteens were checked. All the preparation of these two days meant we'd be in battle sometime soon.

When the word came down that our first stop was Fort Henry, it all made sense. Sail to Fort Henry, then march to Fort Donelson, inching ever closer to Corinth. But the size of the prize would surely dictate the ferocity of the Confederate defense.

We began the march to our riverboats on the 20th of March. Three Iowa Regiments, including ours, were heading south. Union cavalry flanked the flotillas on either shore as we sailed towards Fort Henry, to protect us against attacks by Confederate partisans.

When we arrived after a day and overnight boat trip, our Company Commander, Major Stone, gave us a day of rest before pushing on to Fort Donelson. Fort Donelson. We continued our travel by steamboat. I was glad when our scouts advised that Fort Donelson, now safely in the care of the Iowa 2nd Infantry, was in sight. We march up from the Tennessee river at Pittsburg landing on April 4th.

Our camps were set amid swamps and creeks. Parts of the Army of Tennessee, as we were now known, camped miles away, with our overall commander, General U. S. Grant's headquarters even farther away at Savannah. Here we would wait to rendezvous with General Buell and his Army of Ohio. Then, with our ranks swollen to 54,000, we would begin our last march to assault Corinth. But where we actually fought might be of the enemy's choosing.

Composite of Generals from Finch's' GAR Record

5.   The Battle of Shiloh

Pittsburg Landing, Tennessee April 6-7th

The best laid schemes o' mice an' men gang aft agley.
Robert Burns

Marching southwest on April 3rd, the farther we went, the worse the weather got. It had rained every day so far in April. Our cluster of camps was as muddy as the roads had been on our march. The wool uniform I wore hadn't been dry since we departed Fort Donelson. If there was any redemption at all, we were not being shot at.

The six of us were all in Company F. Amos, Bill, Dan and I stayed together in 1st platoon. The Evans brothers went into 2nd Platoon. As we marched along, our platoon sergeant encouraged any song that came to someone's lips. Every voice in Company F who knew the tune should join in. Ability to sing? Not required.

Soon everybody knew all the words to the oft-repeated tunes: *When Johnny Comes Marching Home; The Battle Cry of Freedom; John Brown's Body; The Girl I Left Behind Me.* The songs lifted our spirits and perhaps for moments helped us forget where we were going and what was yet to do.

The Evans boys split their evenings between our small fire and their new friends in 2nd platoon. I went to sleep, lulled by the music from campfires that clustered near ours.

* * *

It was a different tune, musket fire at a distance, that woke me. But at least the sun shone. It was early, maybe 5:30 or 6, when the bark of bugles forced us from our bedrolls. I elbowed Dan, as he slept face down on the improvised pillow of his uniform jacket.

"Dan, wake up". In the half light of our tent, I fumbled for my hobnailed brogans. We'd slept in the damp wool of our uniform pants and cotton shirts.

Outside, sergeants were running between the rows of tents. Their message, "Up and at 'em boys, the rebs are attacking! Form up, form up!"

"Sergeant, what's happening?" I asked.

"The rebels charged out of the forest at the little Shiloh church and fell upon one of our camps. We've pulled back to organize our defense. There're thousands of 'em on the attack. We're going to help."

The sounds of distant guns increased, undeniably moving ever closer. Neither of us spoke as we grabbed up our belts with their attached gear. I left my wool blanket where it had fallen onto my ground sheet and scrambled outside, Dan close on my heels. The strap of my haversack went over my shoulder so as not to interfere with getting to cartridges and caps.

Muskets from two adjacent tents leaned together outside for the night. Amos and Bill, having emerged first, passed our weapons over. We pocketed the wood tompion plugs used to keep the barrels dry.

Our eighty paper cartridges were safe in two carry pouches, protected inside and outside by leather flaps. Well-greased nitrite flash paper covered the powder and Minié balls. Even amid the approaching sounds of battle, I appreciated that our new muskets were cap lock firings. Water had no effect on the fulminate inside the cap. Everywhere I looked, sergeants were rousing their platoons.

"Form up. Line up. Gear up, load em' up, boys," came their mantra. Our own Sergeant, Ben Lakin, had us in two parallel lines outside our tents. Down the line, I could now see officers moving our way, pointing and speaking just inches from the sergeant's faces. Having their orders heard was crucial.

Seeing order emerging from chaos, his platoon outside and formed up, Sgt. Lakin spoke his order loud and clear, repeating it three times as he pivoted to be heard by all.

"Follow me, lads. Two columns now." He led us out of the tent camp, past our cook fires, tents and tables, toward the open ground behind, which was our assembly point. Following close behind us came David and Jonathan with 2nd platoon. Our march stopped and all 100 men of Company F turned to face the front.

Side by side, all ten companies of the 3rd Iowa Infantry waited in silence. On our left, the 13th Iowa Infantry. On our right, the 2nd Iowa. Six regiments of Iowa infantry stood together. In charge of us all was Col. James Tuttle, the hero of Fort Donelson. He spoke out, loud and clear, from astride his bay horse. More junior officers on their mounts chevroned out beside him.

"Men of Iowa, we will be the center of the line for General Prentiss. The Tennessee River will be on our backs. The rebels face a ravine at their front, while we command the high ground and have the protection of a sunken road. First, we stop the rebels' advance. Then we'll turn the day from his to ours. You trust in God, and I trust in all of you. God bless the Union." A cheer rose from the ranks and the body turned as one and marched off by company.

Our 3rd Iowa infantry stood still in formation as the units around us marched off. Momentarily, I wondered why the 3rd was not joining our other Iowa brethren. My mind was snapped back to the coming fight as an unknown Commanding Officer was about to speak. Sergeants and officers signaled for silence. Our own officer, Major Williams, also on horseback, was positioned just behind the Commander. Now on our left, two Regiments of Illinois Infantry.

"Gentlemen, I am General McClernand. Welcome. Our job today will be to hold the left flank of the Union line. Everyone in Union blue is a brother today," and then the general paused. "And I am proud to be leading you forward. Our position is already scouted. Three companies will go into the line first, because our fighting front is narrowed by a ravine that will slow the rebels' attack.

"The rest of you will go forward as needed. To our Iowa brothers, I say this: you'll not be sacrificed to save Illinois lives. First to go will be two Illinois companies, 29th and 32nd, then the 3rd Iowa.

"Now, let's go kill some rebels."

It was 7: 30 according to my pocket watch. Then came the order, and we wheeled our ranks around and headed out to meet our fate.

* * *

Ahead, I saw the place where we would fight and perhaps die. The road to our appointed spot ran alongside a peach orchard enclosed by a four-foot-high split-rail fence. The orchard was large, filled with mature trees, and every tree was in full bloom. As we marched past this wall of bright pink blooms, the air was perfumed by delicate aromas that called my mind back to honey and almond cake at my mother's table.

Union Troops Marching to the Peach Orchard at Shiloh.

In front of the orchard, another road intersected our route and beyond that lay a large open field. It smelled of newly cut hay. Stubble from the cutting had grown back to a foot tall carpet. Behind the field, ringing it on three sides, stood a thick forest. The trees hid the rebels.

Major Williams placed all ten companies of the 3rd infantry in the center of the Union line. Our backs were to the sun. The split rails of the fence offered scant cover from the lead that would surely be flying our way with deadly purpose. But the rails, for as long as they stood, made an excellent rest for our muskets. I knew that my own aim would be improved by not having to hold aloft the ten-pound weight of my Springfield.

Sergeants, some known and others new to me, paced behind our line. Beyond the one hundred yards of the fence line, to the right of the orchard, was a thick forest. But the enemy was nowhere to be seen. The Iowa 3rd stood alone at the orchard fence, at least for the moment.

Dan Daniels kneeled by my side. I thought I recognized Amos and Bill amid the blue line that extended to my right. Where the Evans boys would fight was not visible to me. I guessed somewhere farther on the right end of our line, in or near the forest. On my left, past the turn of the fence, another company of Union blues was blocking the road down which we'd arrived.

I turned to Dan and tapped his sleeve with the back of my hand. "Let's eat."

He smiled in agreement and we both leaned our muskets against the rails and took off our haversacks. Inside, we found our stock of emergency rations: dried beef, hardtack biscuits and hard candy. Still deeper inside the sack were small rubber bags of salt, pepper, and a stash of cigars. I put down the waterproof sack as a combination kneeler and tablecloth. Eating the dry beef and biscuits was slow work, and only the canteen water made it possible.

I had just returned the extra rations to my bag when off in the near distance, just out of sight, came the sound of marching feet. Over an hour had passed since our arrival and positioning on the line.

How the battle joined on our right by Col. Tuttle and his 2nd Infantry fared was unknown to us. Undoubtedly, our officers knew, but for good or ill, they didn't reveal anything. Still, the constant sound of distant battle, shots by the thousands and cannons booming out by the hundreds, spoke volumes. My watch showed 9:00 in the morning.

National Park Service Battle Site Marker at Shiloh

Across the hundred yards of the hayfield, the sound of drums and bugles added to the rhythm of marching feet. There they were: men in gray or butternut with the morning sun glinting off their musket barrels. Uncounted men emerged from the wood and formed up into lines. They closed and dressed their ranks, drums and bugles silent now. I could see their officers striding before the line. Checking equipment. Giving instruction or encouragement? I'd never know. But I did know they could see us, set and waiting. Yet they seemed splendid and resolute, standing still and waiting patiently in the face of death.

Then it all changed. Confederate officers began shouting and waving their hats above their heads as the lines moved into a double-time advance across the open field. By ten, the battle had truly begun. All our eyes watched the advancing hoard.

Behind our ranks, the sergeants paced. Their mantra began: "Get ready, fix bayonets, check your muskets, hold your fire." These calm, familiar directions from men who'd fought before helped me keep fear from running wild in my head. With my bayonet locked under my musket barrel, I put a compression cap on the musket's nipple, and I was ready. Turning to Dan, I smiled. He nodded back, as no words seemed to fit the uncertainty for either of us.

* * *

Straight across the mown field, directly into our waiting guns, they charged. On they came, their officers on horseback and the uncounted infantry following, spurred on by their own 'rebel yells.' White puffs of smoke from the muzzles of their guns partially covered their advance, their massed fire creating a moving smoke screen.

Behind our ranks, kneeling behind the rail fence, crouched our sergeants. Their mantra now shortened to a single-word chant, "wait---wait---wait". I could see the rebel faces now, charging ever closer, each beard or mustache distinct to its owner.

And then it came, loud and clear, from the massed voices of twenty separate sergeants; "Fire---fire---fire."

And we did, our muskets spewing in a tremendous volley, all down our protective fence line. A hundred men dropped at once, screams mixed with their rebel yells. The following ranks now leapt over the bodies of wounded comrades, slowed but not stopped. Smoke from our guns mixed with their powder smoke as they neared. The air filled with the sharp rotten egg smell from the black powder until the stink dominated my senses.

Our sergeants, now with pistols in hands, paced the line behind us. Their mantra changed now; "shoot while your neighbor loads, nice and steady now boys." Their pacing interrupted only when a trooper needed help with his musket or his nerves. They gave quiet words of reassurance.

Six times the Confederates came, always with their rebel yells and bugles sounding the charge. Each time our lines held, and the rebs were thrown back. But at a terrible cost. Men all around me were hit by Confederate lead. Their muskets, like ours, fired the heavy Minié balls. Each ball, a solid ounce and a half of lead, had the force to blast the life from any flesh it struck.

The wounded, on both sides of the fence, either lay where they fell or made pitiful attempts to crawl away from the oncoming fire. Most of the Confederate wounded suffered and died where they fell.

Even when there were no gray coats advancing, their stream of fire only lessened, but never stopped. This was as quiet as it got, just fewer bullets or more bullets, never complete silence. During the lulls, by the ones or twos, men left the line to help pull our wounded back out of harm's way.

* * *

A field hospital had been set up, one of the sergeants told me. I took my turn helping a wounded comrade off the line. The location of the wound meant he needed only one of us. When the enemy would come again was never known, and every one of our guns would be needed to stop 'em when they came.

As I helped one of the Illinois 29th back to the field hospital, a stream of Union troops was coming to our aid. General McClernand had called on his reserves. Nearing our firing line, the platoons dispersed in twos and threes, replacing our dead and wounded.

I heard and smelled the field hospital before I saw it. The rotten egg smell of the gun smoke changed to something else. The cries, the screams of wounded men, whether waiting for help or going under the knife, filled the air with the audible tune that accompanied the metallic smell of blood. Blood was everywhere. Their torn uniforms and bandages reeked of it. It puddled on the ground and was constantly being sluiced by orderlies off a score of operating tables. A bucket of water tossed on the surgeon's table to wash away the blood was all that separated one patient from another.

I could only watch this butcher's yard for a moment. The Illinois soldier I'd brought in was taken by an orderly, whose pants and shirt were already stained red. My unnamed brother took his place in the queue of wounded awaiting help. As I turned to walk away, my eyes closed, and I willed them to stay shut. This was worse than being on the line.

A tap on my shoulder roused me from my trance. Amos Holt stood in front of me. He was helping Bill Wenger to the doctors. Bill had been hit in the upper left arm. A broken white length of bone protruded through the mangled cloth of his jacket. Blood had already soaked his sleeve, dark red from elbow to cuff.

33

Bill's eyelids fluttered with every footfall, but he uttered not a sound. All I could hear above the sounds of muskets and the cries of the wounded was my own heavy breathing. We led our wounded comrade to a place in the queue. Bill lay down on an empty stretcher, waiting his turn on the great mandala of wounded.

* * *

The sounds of gunfire behind us called Amos and me back to the line. As I turned silently away from Amos, outside the field hospital I saw a quartermaster's supply wagon. I needed cartridges and so did Dan, our first pouch of forty long fired. I yelled back, "Amos, over here, supplies!" He was quick to join me.

A Corporal, in unbloodied blue, supervised the supplies. I picked up three of the wooden pouch inserts of pre-greased powder and lead cartridges. With my free hand, I also took a fresh canteen.

I wished Amos luck, then headed back to my spot on the rail fence and passed cartridges to Dan. The field had gone quiet. Too quiet. Finally, a fearsome storm broke.

Hundreds of gray figures rose up from the low stubble in the hayfield. Their line was no more than twenty yards away from the dirt road that separated the orchard from the field. One mounted figure riding a gray horse rode rapidly forward and out in front of the charging line. Every gray-clad body charged, bayonets gleaming, their silence as ominous as their yells. Our line answered with musket fire and with canister shot from our cannons, placed fifty feet behind our covering infantry. Again, their guns clouded the air with their smoke and smell. And for the first time, I got the sour smell of sweat from the hundreds of dirty wool uniforms.

Union artillery at the Peach Orchard

Their quiet and speed allowed many to make it to our line, where sergeants backed us with their revolvers. Our line began to bend but didn't break, and thus we managed to hold long enough for the rebels to break and withdraw. Their leader must have lived a good Christian life, because though bullets whizzed around him, none took him from his horse.

Now a new enemy appeared where the fence line ended, and our skirmishers were defending the forest. I smelled the wood smoke before I saw the flames. Somehow the forest had ignited, perhaps fed by the dry brush of its understory or fallen dead trees. Out of the crackling sounds of the visible yellow flames came screams from men, their uniforms ablaze.

Confederate sharpshooters waited beyond the hay field for any of us to rise up. Their shots were deadly. We dared not stand and run out to help. To do so was suicide.

Those Union men trapped by the flames, suffering the tortures of hell, fell and rolled to put out the flame or tried to make it to our fence line. More than a few who emerged from the burning forest, fell to rebel sharpshooters, their screams not heard above the screams from within the burning woods. Wounded and unable to move, they died a horrible death.

* * *

It was midafternoon when they came again. This time the Confederate advance was preceded by massed cannon fire. Canister rounds of lead balls tore through men and fence alike. Thirty yards behind the marching cannon fire, the Confederate infantry came, their ranks somehow reinforced. This time our line broke, and a gap separated our men in the orchard from our brothers, defending the road or anchoring the far corner of our right flank.

We retreated and regrouped amid the blooming peach trees, first once and then again deeper into the orchard, next to our cannons. What cover there existed came from the trees and the white powder smoke from our guns. It hung above us, stayed as a blanket, held down by the soft covering quilt of pink blossoms.

The Confederate guns turned trees into sticks, and splinters from broken stumps began to fly besides lead. The pink blossom cover above us was soon shredded and our powder smoke disbursed. The "U" shape of our defensive line kneeled to fire, taking any cover we could from what remained of the trees.

I glanced at Dan, afraid that here we'd both die. But then a hail of fire from behind announced reinforcements, and I hoped for rescue. Fresh troops set a skirmish line, firing and then advancing as the rebels retreated back through the once beautiful orchard, now all destroyed. The four companies had fallen back to make our last stand. Our Iowa 3rd, the two Illinois companies who'd we started together with, and another Illinois, resumed our places along the ruined fence.

I paused and emptied my canteen. I could have drunk a river, but would have settled for dirty water from a horse's hoofprint. I checked my pocket watch: 5:30 now, nine and a half hours since we'd entered the field. The Confederates came no more. As I waited, we were joined by more reinforcements, Iowa boys from the 13th Iowa Infantry.

At 6 PM, the sergeants asked for volunteers to go into the forest to help remove any surviving wounded or the dead. Dan and I both volunteered. Blankets came up from the rear supply wagons for us to use either to carry out the wounded or to remove the dead.

The fire still smoldered amid the remaining blackened trees. We found no survivors, only the dead. These were mostly burned black, beyond recognition, their faces reduced to black ash coating the skull. Those who'd surrendered their lives to the flames grimaced in a macabre smile of gritted teeth, now uncovered by missing lips.

Sometimes bits of metal, perhaps buttons or belt buckles, had fallen into the remains. Those bodies not burned to ash disintegrated to our touch. Only a few could be turned over. Unburned haversacks, scraps of clothing or a cherished cross gave some clue to their identity.

When I turned the body over, I didn't yet know whose remains they were. I called for Dan to come as soon as I opened the haversack that the soldier had saved with his body. Inside among the scraps of rations lay letters and a well-used bible. Inside the cover of the bible, was an inscription.

"May God bless and keep you safe, as you go forth to do the Lord's work." It was signed "Robert Evans."

I passed the open Bible to Dan. "Is that…?"

My question was answered by Dan's query. "Which one?"

I looked at the pack of letters, tied together by a thin purple ribbon. The remains were those of Jonathan Evans. However, the way the fire's course had run, Jonathan's body had not been badly burned. His clothes protected beneath legs and torso got charred but not destroyed. We lifted his remains onto our blanket and lay the haversack on the bones of his rib cage. The strap that had kept the sack behind Jonathan's back was burned away.

We rolled the folded blanket into an improvised stretcher and left the forest with our friend's body. Behind our line, in the twilight of this long April day, a wagon had come up and soldiers were loading our dead for removal.

A young lieutenant, his uniform unmarked by the day, oversaw the wagon. We identified our friend and gave what information we could to help reach his family back in West Union. Jonathan's blanket shroud was then tied together with a rope across chest and ankles. Our identifiers were entered on a numbered card affixed with string to one of the ropes and his name, unit and burial tag number entered into a ledger the lieutenant maintained.

* * *

The Union line stayed in place that night, lest the Confederates attempt another surprise attack. All night our ranks were swollen by reinforcements from General Buell's army. Union and rebel alike slept under constant rain and thunderstorms. Chilling my soul even more was the duty of finding David Evans and telling him his brother was gone.

At 6 AM on April 7th, it was our turn to surprise the enemy. Our ranks had swollen to 54,000 men, with fresh troops from the armies of Generals Buell and Wallace. The rebels, their reserves used up, attempted only two advances before abandoning the field at 2 PM. I learned later that they had withdrawn back to Corinth, Mississippi, our own long-intended battle site.

6.   After the Battle

April 8-16, 1862

Before we rested, the battlefield had to be cleared of the dead. Dan and I had been helping with the scorched remains of those who succumbed to the flames. Other troops, mostly from the relief companies, set to the larger task of clearing the battlefield.

Checking for wounded men still on the field, they removed our men via stretchers and wagons to the medical tents in our rear areas. Enemy wounded suffered different fates. If determined to be mortally wounded, they were left to lie where they fell. We shot some badly wounded as an act of kindness. Others were shot as an act of revenge.

Union dead at the peach orchard went to their final rest in graves dug where they'd fallen. Confederate dead were piled up and burned. Had they not abandoned the field and retreated to Corinth, we would have allowed them to retrieve their own dead.

We salvaged what we could from the field. Muskets, cartridge and cap pouches, canteens, even brogans. We wouldn't waste anything that we might cry for later. Our men didn't stop until all our dead had been laid to rest and the field otherwise cleared.

Dan and I knew the tasks that remained for us. David had to be told, and a letter to the family written. Neither of the two tasks was easier than the other, nor was Dan or I better suited to one task or the other. In the end, we flipped a coin. I lost and the duty of telling David fell to me.

The grave detail lieutenant said our dead from the battle line on our right flank, now being called the "Hornet's Nest," were to be buried in the Shiloh church yard. We agreed to never tell David about how Jonathan died. Dan and I carried mental images no man needed to carry forever after.

I waited until the morning of April 9th, figuring that Jonathan was safe at rest and gone from view. I told David and placed his brother's Bible and letters in his hands. Bending the truth seemed a kindness, perhaps to us both. David said he'd write the letter home, thus sparing Dan the task.

Monument to Iowa Regiments at Shiloh Visitors Center.

Union generals had learned a hard lesson about Confederate tactics. Our camps now maintained strong perimeter guard posts. Beyond these defenses, a steady stream of patrols scoured the countryside for any signs of another sneak attack.

Inside our camp, I was only one of the many naked or half-naked men, wearing perhaps only our boots, that lounged about. As a group, we smelled terrible from the accumulated sweat and bodily waste caked on many a hairy backside. I had no doubt that our collective smell could gag a goat. Gradually, our platoons were allowed to clean ourselves in the nearby Tennessee River.

Blissful rest now, on the heels of the battle. Dan and I finally got back to our pup tent and bedding. As best we could, like everyone else in camp, we tried to dry out ourselves and our uniforms. Now, with our enemy back on his heels, uniforms hung from every natural or improvised hanger. Pants and jackets dried on branches or lay draped over every tent, thin vapors of steam rising to the sky from occasional items.

Major-General Halleck, Commander-in-Chief

Our overall commanding general, Henry Halleck, made preparation for taking the fight to the Confederates at Corinth, Mississippi. General Buell's troops, who'd come to our rescue late on April 6th, continued to pour in. New camps spread out along the edges of our space. Still more men came into our camp. All we knew often came from hearing, then seeing new regiments march in.

I shouted my question out to the newcomers as they marched by, hoping for some grains of information from whomever might reply. "Where are you boys from? What unit are you?" Or, a simple, sincere welcome shout to all who came to march with us.

Besides Sherman's and Grant's troops that had survived, General Buell brought the Army of Ohio. General Thomas and his Army of Tennessee followed in the days to come. Finally, our force was completed by General Pope and the Army of Mississippi. The total size of our assemblage, I can only guess. A hundred thousand men didn't seem to me beyond what I saw and heard.

In a short few days, the largesse that had been accorded men fresh from battle was replaced by the regular order of camp life. At least our uniform, brogans and bedding were finally all dry.

One platoon at a time went to the quartermaster's wagon and refitted with anything we'd lost. Muskets that had last been used as clubs and now had broken firing locks, hammers or nipples got traded out. Canteens, haversacks and all their contents were there for the taking, no questions asked.

Uniform trousers and tunics, if badly torn by shot or shell, were replaced. What I saw was the repair, rearming and refitting of an entire army, including artillery and cavalry.

* * *

Every morning, the pounding of the blacksmith's hammer woke me from my rest. The artillery units, I learned, always traveled with a portable forge, mounted on its own two-wheeled caisson wagon. Iron-rimmed wagon wheels were repaired as needed by the smith or the unit's own carpenters, whose supply wagon traveled with the forge. When my curiosity got the best of me, I asked an artillery man to tell me about their equipment.

"Say friend," I addressed one of the men, who was holding straight a wagon wheel, waiting its turn for repair. "What do you call them parts? The thing the cannon rides on and the two carts with the big chests on top?" When the soldier turned to face me, I extended my hand in a spirit of brotherhood.

"Duane Finch, 3rd Iowa, and you?"

In response, he returned my greeting. "Otis Clapp, 15th Illinois We heard you had the Devil's own time back there at Shiloh." My smile tightened to a grimace, and I kept my answer short.

"We anchored the center of the line at the peach orchard. Their artillery killed a lot of good men. Canister shot."

He made no response, except to nod in recognition of the pain that came with any recall. "I got to keep this here wheel up, but let me point to this and that. Give you their names and how all the puzzle pieces fit together."

Now it was my turn to nod.

"Our cannons are 12-pounders. Same as the rebs have. The cannon rides on a two-wheeled carriage." He pointed to a cannon and carriage parked just a few feet away.

"All right."

"Them two arms of the cannon cart that angle down and in, we call the 'trail.' The trail hooks onto the two-wheeled cart. That cart is called the 'limber' and the box with the metal top is full of

43

ammunition. See, that lifts the cannon cart tail so our six-horse team can pull the gun." Otis paused, waiting for some sign that I understood.

"Okay," I replied.

"Now the last, bigger piece of each crew cannon is called a caisson. The largest two-wheeled wagon. That thing carries two ammunition chests. We load up all our odds and ends: extra wagon wheel, a barrel swab, ramrods, a chest of tools and igniter sticks. We use them to touch to the powder primer hole," said Otis, pointing out each as he spoke.

"Them thar ammunition chests hold about 30 rounds each, explosive ball shot rounds or canister rounds. We try to park the caisson at a safe spot behind the gun. We sure as heck don't want a reb round to hit one of them. We load the gun from the box on the limber and pack rounds up to keep the gun fed."

He must have sensed that no further explanation of either type of round was necessary, nor wanted. I had faced canister and explosive shot, so he stopped talking. We stood silent for a few moments. I thanked him and we parted with exchanged wishes for our own safety. I walked away as Otis finally got the call to roll his wheel up to the battery wagon for repair.

Walking back toward my own camp, I saw horses and mules arriving. Soldiers had not been the only casualties. Replacement cavalry mounts, draft horses and mules to pull scores of wagons were led off to improvised corrals.

The sound of tapping grew louder, and the smell of manure got stronger. Two farriers were busily shoeing the new mounts, using ready-made shoes pulled from a bucket fixed to the side of a supply wagon.

I stopped to watch the work. Behind and to the right, another group of craftsmen was repairing leather horse and wagon tack. One man with a parrot-beak-shaped knife was cutting leather strips. Another trooper operated some kind of large sewing machine that stitched together the folded ends of straps, thus affixing rings or buckles, making the raw materials into functioning harness parts. A third man, swinging a hammer, punched eyelet holes into straps as a final touch.

In eight days, our reequipping, rearming and replacing every regimental space were all accomplished. I was sure that soon our force, now three armies strong, would begin closing on Corinth.

The Mississippi river would no longer be a Confederate waterway if Vicksburg, Mississippi, fell. But to attack Vicksburg, Corinth needed to be taken first.

Rivers and railroad lines had always shaped Union strategy. As rivers were lost by the Confederacy, rails loomed even larger. And Corinth, Mississippi, became the apex of the south's rail system, where two major rail lines crossed.

Rails moved Confederate troops in to defend against 100,000 attacking federals.

7. The Siege of Corinth

April 29-May 30, 1862

We'd made a slow march south from Pittsburg Landing. Our commanding General Harry Halleck moved his three armies cautiously forward. The 3rd Iowa had become part of General Thomas' Army of Tennessee, and General Hurlbut's 4th Division. Our company Commander was Capt. John B. Smith.

Halleck, an engineer by training, chose each night's campsite for its defensive position. A lot of us probably would have been pretty good miners or canal diggers after almost three weeks of entrenching the perimeter of our camps. Before that, I had dug latrine slit trenches but never ditching and building berms. Halleck seemed determined not to be caught unprepared again.

Our supply trains included water wagons as we moved inland from the Tennessee river. For guides, generals relied on local partisans. They knew where along our road springs offered fresh water. The same wagons carried barrels of vinegar, which we used to make the water safe if it began to turn brackish. Awful to drink, but better than going without or suffering from foul water.

Finally, our unmolested march stopped on April 28th. We approached Corinth as the right wing of our force, General Buell in the center and Pope on the left. The Confederates had set up a series of defensive positions at every crossroad or town. They fought to keep Corinth safe.

Union Troops Fighting at Corinth

First cavalry fought in the little area called Monterey. It wasn't more than one day more when our boys on the left wing fought and captured the town of Farmington. Corinth was now in sight. Our fight with the defensive outposts of Corinth came on May 16th.

* * *

We waited as the ready reserve, staged up behind the right flank of our Union line. The rebs were dug in. They had trenches ahead of their earthen palisades. Log barricades topped each defensive position. The stout wood barriers were simple and ingenious. Even from our vantage point some distance behind the attack, their construction was clear.

First two stout logs went down, their butts facing forward. Then one log was laid on top directly over the earthwork crest and secured in place. They had perhaps a six-inch high gap between earth and log as a clear rifle port. Confederates could shoot from behind the earthen and log barrier. Our shots had to thread the six-inch gap to even have a chance at scoring a hit.

General Hurlbut's men made slow, if any progress, pinned down by Confederate fire and deterred from making a bayonet charge by the well-constructed defensive line. The left wing of our attack faced heavy fire from Confederates in and around a farmhouse. Finally, our superior numbers and resources began to assert themselves.

From our rear came Otis Clapp's 15th Illinois artillery and their guns fanned out to a firing line in front of us. The rebel defenses and determination faltered and collapsed under the barrage from the Illinois guns. Artillery turned the battle, and the Confederate lines broke.

They made their last stand at the log farmhouse, late in the day. Our losses were light, and the Iowa 3rd finally joined the battle as the last of the rebs abandoned the log house. Most of the Confederates had withdrawn from this hilltop position. Now our Union guns would have the high ground and a view that overlooked Corinth.

*　*　*

With their outer defenses so well prepared, we got ready to assault the Corinth rail junction. Every day now, in ones and twos, gray-clad soldiers began to appear under white flags with raised arms, hoping to surrender. After checking them for hidden weapons, we marched them back to our commanders.

Trading news for clemency, they told of being issued three days' rations, extra ammunition, and being told to be ready for a counterattack. There was also sickness in the camp.

General Halleck ordered us to fortify our front with palisades of our own. Again, Dan and I joined the ranks of diggers. We worked under the watchful eyes of the covering infantry, ready to respond to any Confederate surprise. So began a slow march forward.

Each day we advanced a little, gaining positions and choosing our battlefield. Each day ended the same, with new fortifications for our line. Speed was sacrificed for safety, and that was fine with me. Now the sounds of the Confederate camp became audible. In the distance we heard occasional cheers, often preceded by what might have been the puffing and clatter of steam engines.

"Sounds to me like they're cheering the arrival of fresh troops. What do you think, Dan?"

He responded with a shrug. By the 28th, we were no more than 1000 yards from the rail junction. Our scouts crept closer. Finally, on May 29th, we entered Corinth. The Confederates had fled. What had sounded like reinforcements to us had been a clever retreat. But they lived to fight another day.

THE REBEL FLEA.
You put your Finger on him, and he isn't there.

8.   The Journey to Vicksburg Begins:

Hatchie River Bridge, October 1862

Well, I'll be dipped in shit; the rebs are trying to take back Corinth.

General Halleck decided to split up his armies after Corinth. The Army of Ohio got sent up to occupy Nashville. We stayed part of Grant's Army of Tennessee and set to work repairing the railroads at Corinth. Under constant cover from our forward scouts and picket lines of guard posts, we worked.

Where our artillery had blown up tracks, shell craters needed filling, then ties, and rails replaced. When our work was done, the captured rail lines connected with other secure Union rails. Supplies now flowed in more easily and our severely wounded out to hospitals at Fort Leavenworth, St. Louis or further north.

I thought finally we might get a rest and something of a refit when, in the third week of July; we marched into Memphis. And refit we did. Supplies came down the river and overland. For the first time in weeks, I was clean and eating hot food. Then word came down the line. We'd be moving out in a few short days.

On September 6th our Fourth Division headed east. In three days, we arrived at Bolivar, Tennessee. There we stayed until October 3rd when word came that the Confederates were trying to retake Corinth. So back we marched! We quick marched with little rest, not wanting to give back the prize so recently purchased with Union blood.

* * *

We met the rebs at the Hatchie river bridge on October 5th. Capt. Trumbull from 'B' Company led us as we fought our way across the bridge. It was our turn to meet the type of obstacles the rebs had faced at Shiloh. Instead of them fighting through brush to charge up a hill, we charged uphill into enemy fire. And ours was a steeper hill to climb than the one they'd faced at Shiloh. Our equivalent of brush to fight through was crossing an uncovered bridge.

Men I knew by sight and many by name, quick-marched across the bridge. The Confederate earthen and log rampart was ahead and above us. Shooting up and at them was near impossible. The time to stop, aim, and fire only made each of us a better target. So I didn't reload until I was across. Speed was our best weapon and defense.

The soldier at my side suddenly convulsed, his arms flinging wide as the impact of the Confederate ball radiated shock through his system. And down he fell, blocking my path. He screamed no words, just cries. I bent and worked to free my feet and legs from his weight; all too quickly quiet, dead weight now.

Then the soldier behind me was hit. Forward he fell and the ten pounds of his musket crashed onto the side of my head, stinging my right ear. I heard no scream, just the gurgle of blood oozing from his throat. His head rested on his bloody chest, as he no longer had a spine to carry its weight.

Just for a moment, I was pinned by the bodies of fallen comrades. My empty head, now shouting to my conscious mind, *Lie down between the bodies. Hide, wait, play dead!* From someplace within myself, welled up, *Go-go-go; run-run; Get off the bridge.*

And I did. From lying amid our dead, to kneeling and rising to a crouch, I half-ran forward. Stepping over bodies of the fallen, all I could see through a narrowed tunnel of vision was the far bank of the Hatchie and our line of riflemen firing up into the rebels.

Next to me was Lt. Foote, already wounded in the forearm. His musket cast aside, pistol in hand, he led our charge. "Follow me," were his last words to reach my ears over the buzzing of musketry and the shouts of our troops. The shot that took the lieutenant in the chest raised the fabric of his tunic's back. As the cloth of his uniform coat settled against his fallen form, the jacket bloomed red. I neither stopped nor looked again as a shot blew my cap from my head.

Those of us who made it across took to any available cover and tried to keep Confederate fire off those men still crossing. Finally, our officers signaled for our line of battle to move against the high ground straight ahead.

To stop was surely to die. The first of us to reach the crest of the hill through the puffs of powder smoke, shot and then bayonetted the men in gray. As their fire slowed, our fight at their line changed into single combat. Bayonets were our lances, and muskets our clubs. It didn't matter to me. I was going to kill as many of them as I could before they killed me.

The call of their bugles sounding retreat got lost amid the panting of our exhausted men. But the rebels heard the sound and began to turn and flee the line into the covering woods behind. The few of us with strength enough to shoot probably did. For myself, I couldn't bring myself to shoot a fleeing enemy in the back even if he'd been trying to kill me. My knees collapsed and down I went. But even then, my hands and arms operated by memory to charge my musket and aim towards the woods.

As our ranks filled, my mind went to black, passed out or lost to sleep, and for how long, I never determined. I woke with a start. "What?" I verbalized to no one as my mind came awake. Lying next to me was our own F Company leader, Captain Aaron Brown.

"They've all hooked it; gone," he said. He patted my shoulder as he rose. "Keep watching the wood." He moved down the hilltop line, checking on his men, giving praise and orders as he moved.

Behind and below where I lay, in the butcher's yard on the bridge and opposite riverbanks, they began counting the dead and removing the wounded. I counted 62 lifeless bodies laid together side by side, awaiting their final wagon ride. Shoulder to shoulder with other Iowa men, we waited for relief or attack. For how long the wait, none of us knew.

Finally, relief arrived in the form of new blue-clad bodies. They filled the tamped down ground we'd shaped and warmed. I staggered down the hill, picking up a kepi cap from the ground where it lay. Under heavy guard, we bivouacked. Those of us with enough strength left, put up our two-man pup tents, spread ground cloths and collapsed under our blankets with haversack pillows. It was good to be alive.

I'd never felt so alone and vulnerable, even as one of many, while charging that hill. Lying there in the half-light, I searched myself for an emotion. I wasn't mad at the rebels or our officers, just sad perhaps. It was good to be alive and not alone.

* * *

We took winter quarters at Moscow, Tennessee, to rest, rearm, resupply, and refill our ranks.

Arriving in mid-November after another long march, every man of us was bone tired. Rest was the only cure for the multitude of pains that plagued us as we marched along.

Thanksgiving at Camp

The unions' quartermaster corps was ready and waiting for us in Moscow. Whatever we needed in supplies sat there for replacement or exchange. All of us refilled every pouch and replaced the broken, lost, or battered.

I traded my ragged uniform coat for new. What I got had its own tale to tell if it could only speak. Under the right sleeve was a repaired bullet hole. Union resources vastly exceeded those of the Confederacy in everything from brogan shoes up through uniforms to muskets. But my new coat, recycled from another soldier, showed that even supplies were not inexhaustible.

There were packages and letters from home waiting there or continually arriving, and we all had our own letters to send. We had survived. Mom sent pairs of socks and union suit drawers.

She had anticipated the box's long journey. She'd sent only treats that would neither spoil nor grow stale. There were two paper-wrapped fruitcakes. Each cake had long been soaked by generous amounts of brandy being poured on and allowed to join the raisins, nuts and candied fruit that filled the cakes. She used just enough sweet brown ginger cake to bind all the goodies together.

The 3rd Iowa was a veteran unit now. All of us, especially our leadership, had learned from every lesson that we had managed to survive. As November turned into December, wool topcoats were issued. Praise God! The New Year passed and heralded the arrival of replacements for those we'd lost. President Lincoln now began drafting eligible men.

* * *

They came with little to no enthusiasm for the Union cause. Our new regimental commander, Capt. Aaron Brown, was now Major Brown, promoted for his bravery at the Hatchie bridge. He wisely took a different approach. Unlike our first days in uniform, there was a plan for the new men, draftees all. He was matter-of fact in his explanation of why they needed to listen and learn.

"Beginning tomorrow, you'll be assigned to fill spots in 1st or 2nd platoon in F Company. Your teachers will be men who've survived twenty months of war. Among other things, they will teach you to load and fire your musket. We will teach you how to shoot and hit your target. How to march and follow directions to move, or stand, or retreat, all in good order. We fight as a unit and live together as one."

Then Maj. Brown paused and ran his eyes down the line of his new men before going on. "It seems to me that you have two choices. You can run away, first chance you get. When we find you, and we will, we hang deserters," and again he paused. "Or you can listen to what we'll teach, which will help you stay alive. If you do that, you'll have one hundred brothers fighting alongside you."

His "come to Jesus" speech done, he turned the new arrivals over to Sgt. Lakin, who formed the replacements into a single line and began placing them in front of the empty or half full tents that dotted our company area. One filled the Evans boy's place in 2nd platoon.

54

Bill Wenger's loss had long ago been filled, so only two of the new men were put into spots near Dan and me.

George Erickson from Milwaukee and Leo McCarthy from Chicago joined our campfire that night. Our collective job was to turn these raw recruits into fighters who we could trust at our side. So, it began, the passing of culture, the thousand little things that had kept us alive.

Their days were filled with marching, musketry and close quarter fighting with bayonet and rifle butt. Practice taught them how to load, fire, and reload again. The culture of surviving in battle came not only on the drill field or at the rifle range, but around our eight-man campfire.

"Breathe steady. Don't rush or you waste a shot. Aim while your neighbor reloads. You are never too tired to clean your musket or fill your cartridge and cap pouches. Keep that canteen full of sweet, fresh water."

With sticks instead of bayonets, they learned how to thrust, parry and use a butt strike. "Don't listen to the rebel yells. Shoot from a rest or kneeling if you can. Don't panic, don't run and don't worry about what we can't change." Then it was time to end training and break camp. Our men would move by the river, thankfully.

9. Ambush on the River

Jackson, Mississippi, July 1863

There were a thousand of us packed onto the *Crescent* as she steamed down the Wolf River to join Grant's army. Her one-hundred-fifty-foot wood hull carried two full decks above, with cargo space and her giant boiler below the main deck. Each deck was shaded by the fully railed walkways. Two steel stacks, each crowned with decorative cap pieces, belched smoke continuously. Above the top deck, the wheelhouse sat over the combination office and captain's quarters.

The rebels lay in wait, hidden by the cover of brush and trees that lined the riverbank. Their first shots were well aimed, and the crack of bullets pierced the air. Watching from the rails or sitting on the prow or stern, we made excellent targets, and fourteen of us got severely wounded. At least most of us never let our muskets leave our side.

If there was no immediate cover, men dropped flat onto the deck and prayed, until the worst of the firing subsided. I had my musket and was leaning against the main salon wall, preferring the shade from the second deck's overhang. I kept to the shade as I returned fire, trying to aim for the white puffs of smoke that betrayed their covers.

How many we hit, I still don't know. But as more of us returned fire, theirs faded away, and we sailed past the ambush site. After that, we kept a constant guard, and no one lounged in the open. We only had fifteen more miles to traverse on the Wolf River before we moved on to the Mississippi at Memphis. Now we had the cover of two ironclads from Commodore Foote's squadron. They paralleled our course south, one on either side of our steamer.

Ironclads

By nine o'clock the next morning, we docked at Young's Landing and joined Grant's army. We were placed on the left flank of the Union line and there we began construction of our field fortifications. Palisades with firing steps formed a half-circle around our end position.

"Pascal died." The news came from Tom Wainwright, who manned the adjacent guard post. I tapped the ash off my cigar, remaining careful to keep covered its glowing tip with my opposite hand. The glowing point of red light made a great target for any rebel sharpshooter.

"Who's Pascal" I asked, not recognizing the name. "Pascal Redburn, one of the Fayette boys. The Reb ambush on the Crescent got him." I made no reply and returned to watching the shoreline for a Confederate smoker, whom I might use to even the score for Pascal.

* * *

Few things travel faster in an army camp than news. Truth, rumor or speculation, that was the difference. Our part of the Army of Tennessee joined this great assemblage of fighting men. Boys from the Army of Ohio had been with Grant since the start of the Vicksburg campaign, back in May of '62. We were on our way to join in the assault of Vicksburg.

Seven assaults from different directions hadn't breached their defenses. Stout earthen and wood palisades had been constructed to seal off those avenues of attack not already protected by substantial natural barriers. High bluffs backed the city. Confederate cannons atop the bluffs warded off attacks by river or crossing anywhere within their range. Their cannons and sharpshooters took a daily toll.

I've heard men say, "pick your poison." Usually, they are talking about whiskey or the ever-present soldiers' joy. The same could be said about the part we'd play in trying to take Vicksburg. The agreement around our campfire, or in cook lines was, Vicksburg was worth the taking. But we didn't get to pick our poison.

Vicksburg was the last rebel port on the Mississippi, and hence the last path for supplies in from the west. Its rail hub was the only remaining way to move supplies or men to the Confederate east. And it was one of ever-fewer ports where Confederate blockade runners could try moving cash crops out to European markets. The Union navy had long ago captured the port of New Orleans and established a blockage below Vicksburg. Their food supply was cut.

Part of our army was making a third attempt to descend on Vicksburg from the lightly defended north approach. But the natural defense of the Yazoo River delta created a giant marsh where the Yazoo joined the Mississippi. Alligators, water moccasin snakes and mosquito-borne illness joined the soft ground to make moving men and cannon almost impossible, but still we tried yet again. Failure to take Vicksburg was not an option.

Grant had entire work crews digging canals at a river bend above Vicksburg. If the Mississippi river flow could be diverted, it created new options for attack. No matter how much manpower Grant threw at the task, we were no match for nature. This effort ended up only serving the rebels as we managed to flood a good portion of the northern approach. Never content to accept a failure, he ordered the streams out of the Yazoo delta that supplied the city's water supply diverted. With their food supply and water source both cut off, he waited.

CUTTING THE CANAL OPPOSITE VICKSBURG.—Sketched by Mr. Theodore R. Davis.—[See Next Page.]

We settled into a routine, guarding fixed posts from Confederate attacks on our rear. I supposed that old Ulysses did learn good after Shiloh. He was not going to be ambushed again. We held our post for forty days, waiting for Vicksburg to surrender. And it did on July

4, 1863. Just like at Corinth, the ancient strategy of starving out an enemy worked for us. With the ambush at Pittsburg Landing still burned into Grant's mind, we continued to keep our rear-guard post.

While our collective future was yet to be revealed to us by our commanders, we did have a ringside seat to view the rebel withdrawal from the city. None of us fired even a shot at the broken army that passed us by, marching four abreast. No rebel yells nor singing or bugles now. Nine thousand skinny, ragged men passed in silence. There were no taunts from our men as the enemy shuffled past.

When Maj. Brown next made his routine daily check on our position, I asked what we were seeing. "General Grant chose to parole the Confederate troops. He believed that their condition, when seen by the folks at home, would be more demoralizing than our taking nine thousand prisoners. Each man signed an oath not to take up arms again during the conflict. The soldiers surrendered their muskets and swords, but he allowed them to keep horses and a handgun."

10. Hubris Kills

Jackson, Mississippi, July 12, 1863

Theirs not to reason why...
Tennyson

Our new orders: move across the river and begin a siege of Jackson, Mississippi.

When he arrived, Sherman found the city strongly defended by well-prepared fortifications. To avoid the human cost of a frontal attack, he instead set up our artillery positions, each defended by earthworks and infantry.

Our regiment arrived, and we were ordered forward, with the 3rd Iowa anchoring the south end of the line. Our Commander was Brigadier General Lauman. Word around camp was that Lauman was one of the young fire-breathers. Like newly minted Brigadier General George Custer, who now commanded one of our Michigan cavalry units, Lauman got his battlefield promotion for doing the impossible. By reputation, our leader was fearless, a risk taker who never thought any task was beyond his capacity. What I wanted to know was, did he lead from the front or the rear of the troops? Would he send us to face Confederate lead and steel, protected only by our wool uniforms? Only time would tell.

July 12th began with a heavy cannon barrage on the Confederate positions. Our order was to attack the Confederate lines. Our brigade commander, Col. Pugh, of the Illinois 17th, questioned the advisability of crossing an open field in front of Confederate artillery. BG Lauman then came forward to examine the Confederate front. Dan and I occupied places in the final assault wave. Where we waited allowed us to see and hear the general.

"Col. Pugh, good day sir."

Pugh acknowledged the general and the small retinue of junior officers following obediently behind.

"Col. Pugh, tell me what you see that you believe I might have overlooked." Lauman's words, said with emphasis, sounded like distain to me. Some of the junior officers watched intently for Col.

Pugh's response, others among them appeared to deliberately look away or study their own shoes.

"General, with respect, what I'm seeing from our vantage point here makes approaching that close an unacceptable risk, sir."

"Col. Pugh, let me assure you that Generals Ord, Hovey, and I have considered every possibility. Our own artillery is fully capable of supporting the advance. I trust that Major-General Ord sees a weakness in the rebel lines in your sector."

Then Lauman's tone seemed to soften and with that, he placed a big brotherly hand on Pugh's shoulder. "Men die in war, you know it, I know it. But even more men can die when an opportunity is lost." Both men stood in silence for a while. BG Lauman did an about face and marched his cadre of subordinates off. His final words, delivered as he turned, "So, I'm not about to go against the orders of my superiors…and neither should you.

* * *

"You heard the man. Up and at em' boys," shouted Sgt. Lakin. Col. Pugh had given the order before this discussion and it hadn't been changed after he met the general. Lauman was gone, back to the safety of the rear, but his order remained. We didn't know the general from a "bale ah hay," but our colonel we'd follow, because he led from the front. *Boy, pride is a bitch.*

The width of our section of the Union line set the size of our own advance. As our line formed, it seemed pretty near a hundred yards wide. Major Brown stood back, directing his lieutenants and their sergeants. Ahead of me, I saw four parallel lines of us. Our first line stepped off and began a double time march across the open field that separated us from the enemy. Our second line stepped off twenty yards behind the first, and so it went.

Somewhere out there sat Confederate cannons. I recognized this from the previous days, when our artillery traded shots with theirs. But looking from our line, five hundred yards back, their lines and the supporting guns were little more than blurs or bumps on the far horizon. The three regiments of Illinois infantry on our left had stopped advancing and were busy digging rifle pits.

Dan and Amos walked next to me. We stepped out onto the soft earth that might have been a potato field, with the rest of our fifth line. Something in the air caught my attention. *What the heck?*

"Do you hear that?" I said to no one in particular.

Both Amos and Dan turned toward me, listening now.

"Piano music?" asked Amos.

"I'm hearing singing," said Dan. And there it was, Confederate voices, belting out 'Dixie' to their unseen piano player tickling unseen ivory keys.

Our line moved forward from the precipice into the caldron of battle. As we did, the enemy's muskets opened up with a tap-tap-tap of fire. The buzz of passing shots joined their music. Then came the first cries from boys as rebel shots struck Union flesh. But our blue wave rolled on. Our boys stood to reload, some kneeling to aim and shoot. But we all continued forward, unstopped by the Confederate fire.

And their music played on.

Then the gates of hell flung open. Massed Confederate cannons cut loose with a roar and a huge volley of fire. Canister shot. I knew the sound and witnessed the result as our front ranks slowed, but didn't stop. There was no cover to be had, so on we all went.

As their cannon fire broke into individual guns firing, the screams and curses of our dying and wounded sounded. They blended into a constant din, punctuated by the boom of a cannon or the high-pitched whine of a bullet whizzing past my head.

We had to step over bodies or around our wounded. Their cries for help couldn't be answered. Bloody hands reached out, perhaps grabbing an ankle, and got brushed away. I ran, stopping only to kneel, reload, and fire. If I hit any of them, I have no idea. Their volume of fire, as revealed by puff after puff of smoke, never slowed.

Fewer and fewer blue jackets advanced ahead of me. Men in blue were stopped, taking a tiny bit of cover from a Confederate barrier some eighty yards from their line. A solid wall of blue jackets had no way forward. Unable to advance, some turned and tried to retreat, but those who did died trying.

Somewhere behind me, a bugle was sounding 'retreat.' From where I kneeled, I looked around for my friends. Neither was near me any longer. Killed, wounded or separated, but safe? I could only pray, because I could not wait. I made an unspoken promise to myself that if I found either Dan or Amos somewhere behind me, I'd bring them out with me, living or dead.

The souls I passed lay where they'd fallen. Some face down in the dirt. Others had maneuvered to their back or side before death had overtaken them.

Confederate shots still came our way. Cannon fire still raked the field. The last thing I saw before turning to follow the bugle call was our men stopped at the barrier. They began to put their muskets down and stand up, resigned to surrender.

And their music played on.

* * *

Safe now behind our own lines, past the rifle pits and artillery emplacements, I stopped and fell to my knees. My nostrils were full of the sulfur smell of gunpowder. My musket dropped from my trembling hands. I tried to reach my canteen, but the tremor of my hands only succeeded in getting the cap off before they dropped the water vessel. I watched as the contents spilled out, but neither my hands nor mind seemed able to stop the flow.

Kneeling, safe at last, my mind was unstuck in time, my hearing reduced to a solitary high-pitched ringing in my ears. Then a hand squeezed my shoulder, and I came back to the here and now. There was Dan standing beside me and offering his own canteen. I tried to speak, but only a croak emerged. I took the canteen, drank and passed out.

When I awoke, Dan and Amos were with me. All three of us sat on the ground, our backs against the wheel of an artillery caisson. The words were clear, but I still couldn't identify the speaker at first. "Hey, you had that look in your eye that grown men get when they want to cry. Can you make it if we stand you up? We'll all walk back to camp when you're able. There's hot food and coffee." Dan's voice cut through the ringing in my ears, but I made no reply.

As my mind and body synchronized, the surroundings fell into place and the sounds became recognizable. "Are you hurt?" was my question to both my friends. Among such violence, we three had escaped untouched.

After the fight, generals of the blue and the gray honored a white flag of truce. Both sides were allowed to clear the field of their dead and wounded, since we had not fled the field but merely retreated to our main line of defense.

The 3rd was spared either of these tasks, as ours had been in the fight. So, others from our ranks came to clean the field. Stretchers removed survivors while the dead left by wagon. We watched from our respite as wagon after wagon, stretcher after stretcher passed by. Our dead would be buried elsewhere, since the control of the battlefield was still contested. *Perhaps there is still hope for us all, blue and gray.* I held that possibility in my mind, fed by our mutual respect for the white flag of truce and the removal of our dead.

* * *

Back at our original bivouac, the third ranking officer in command of our regiment assembled us into a formation. Barely two hundred able men answered the roll call, from among the 880 who'd gone into the fight. The regiment suffered 68 killed, 302 wounded and 200 captured. *We damn near fought ourselves out of existence.*

The sounds we began to hear as the three of us walked back to camp told us that the field hospital was ahead and to our right. The too-familiar screams, crying, and moans were inescapable, except by walking farther and faster away.

All at once, there was a roar, and flames leaped into the air. The hospital screams and cries were now mixed with shouting. A new set of high-pitched screams covered everything. Suddenly, running toward us, were two flaming figures. Their faces were contorted by screams. Facial features were gone or going, and the screams, just animalistic cries of unstoppable, unendurable pain.

On they came, hair, skin, and clothing alight until death stopped them. Behind them a wagon blazed on, as men roused from rest came with water and smothering blankets to staunch the flames. While not beyond caring, we knew we were beyond helping there and then. So we walked on. Our tolerance for death was reached for the day.

That night, word came that the fire was an accidental spark igniting a fresh container of the surgeons' ether. The next day, Amos located the officer in charge of identifying our dead comrades. Listed among the names was David Evans.

When Amos shared the sad news, we all agreed that we needed to see his body if it could be located amid the dozens of corpses. In a line of blanket wrapped figures, laid side by side on the ground, we found our friend.

When we opened his burial shroud, we knew David had died quick and clean from a single shot through his forehead. Back around our fire, we rolled dice to determine who would write the letter to his family.

11. Respite: on Leave at Last.

Jackson to Atlanta, July 1863-March 1864

Following the cycle of army life, we withdrew first to Vicksburg, which was still shot up and suffering from disease after the siege. I learned from townspeople how the Union dammed off streams that provided their fresh water. Then disease began to spread. They ate their cattle first, then the horses and mules. Dogs and cats went last, just before the rats, euphemistically served as "squirrel stew." They were forced to leave their homes and seek cover in natural caves beneath the bluffs because of our artillery bombardment.

Soon, wiser or at least kinder souls prevailed, and we moved on to Natchez, Mississippi. There we stayed and rested, refit, and replaced our significant manpower losses over the winter.

Our only action of note was a one-month rebel-hunting trek, in February of '64. We searched over to and then back from Meridian, Mississippi, traveling light without tents or wagons. Our rations ran out, and we scavenged for what we could from the land. The winter rain was miserable, but such is the army.

Back at last in Natchez, many of us found our three-year enlistments were up. A full three-quarters of our regiment reenlisted, agreeing to serve for the duration of the war. In thanks, we were given a thirty-day furlough. This included partial transportation home and our leave did not begin until we arrived there.

* * *

Immediately upon getting the good news, I wrote my parents, giving them my best guess as to travel and arrival times. The letter would probably arrive when I was already on the road. "I expect to be home by March 26th, but don't worry if I'm not. Love, Duane." Dan sent the same news to his wife, and Amos sent the same to his family.

From Dad's maps of Iowa railroads, I guessed that the lines ran mostly east-west. There were some spur lines, but nothing yet connected the east side of Iowa on a north-south axis. Our travel from Davenport north to West Union would have to be by the stage. This was our first trip home in three years.

We boarded a steamer and headed north on the Mississippi, all the way to Davenport. I expected the trip to take four or five days. Depending if anyone took a shot at us or hatched some other rebel bullshit. Our stops for fuel allowed us to send mail and for fresh fruits and vegetables to come on board.

We made no other stops, sailing from first light until it became too dark to keep a watchful eye on the water ahead. I asked a crew member, "Why don't we just sail through the night?"

"Floating logs needed to be avoided. As well, the Confederacy uses explosive mines, which, if struck, could sink us. They also use bombs camouflaged as large lumps of coal to blow up our boilers, so our fueling is necessarily a slow, deliberate process."

The trip was a chance for a well-needed rest. The food got better as fruit, vegetables and fresh-caught fish supplemented the usual soldiers' diet of beef, beans and biscuits. I replenished my supply of cigars at Natchez.

Life was good here and now. Sadder but wiser, I'd learned to only deal with the present. If nothing bad is happening at this moment, leave the future alone. I'd get no comfort from worrying about what might come next.

We pulled into the Davenport dock on the 23rd. We used our carefully preserved letter from Sheriff McPherson and the mayor of West Union at the stage depot, hoping for a deal or discount. Before the station agent could even reply, a well-dressed man going on the same stage offered to pay our fare. Surprised, the agent alternated looks for me to the other man, and back before announcing, "Soldier, you ride for free."

Hiram, our benefactor, was a veteran of the War of 1812, a die-hard abolitionist and now a resident of Milwaukee. We shared war stories from our pasts as we rode along sharing a coach, meals, and lodgings. He gave his assessment of the state of the war and the capacities of our various generals.

Grant had risen to overall command of all the Union forces, and the control of the Confederacy was shrinking daily. He told us the story of Confederate William Cantrell's guerilla raid on Lawrence,

Kansas. He and his men killed two hundred men and boys, simply for being Union sympathizers.

Hiram seemed to think that the public, or at least those not infused with his abolitionist zeal, were growing tired of the war and disliked the draft. He added to our knowledge with details about our great victory at Gettysburg from early July.

The stage stopped at Dubuque for the first night and at Marquette for the second. By noon on the third day, we'd be in West Union. By the time we parted, we were all well acquainted from our traveling conversations.

* * *

Getting off the stage for the final time, I looked around. West Union didn't seem to have changed much. Stepping out and stretching my back, then flexing my knees, I waited for the Gladstone travel bag I'd bought for the round trip to be removed from the luggage boot. The three of us had carried little in the way of personal possessions during our time in the fields.

The station agent stepped out of the office. "Welcome to West Union. We change horses here. You have time for a meal if you like, and you'll be on your way in an hour." Pointing to his left, he continued with other essential information for the travelers.

"The privy is down the walkway on the right side of our office." Then, pointing in the opposite direction, he added, "Just three doors down on the left is the Howard Hotel, where you can purchase a meal if you like. Please be back here by 1 PM."

As the other four passengers separated to the left or right, I found my parents seated on a bench under the porch overhang. By their side was Dan's wife and with her was a small boy, whom I guess had never yet seen his daddy.

Each of us offered greetings to the family members who'd come to the station and confirmed our plan to meet at the stage depot early on April 25th. We'd all go back to the regiment together. Amos waved goodbye and set off to his parents' home.

As I stepped forward, Dad stood up and strode off the porch. We shook hands, one soldier greeting another comrade-in-arms. Back pats and greeting exchanged, I left my bag sitting in the street and stepped onto the sidewalk, reaching out to Mom and wrapping my arms around her.

She must have gotten shorter and lighter, because she weighed next to nothing when I lifted and spun her around. Had I perhaps changed?

Arm in arm, the three of us walked down the street along the single block to the livery, where Dad's buggy waited. Cleopatra, Dad's mule, turned her head and took an indifferent glance before turning to her familiar task. I tossed my bag behind the rear bench seat and helped Mom in. Dad and I took the front seat and off we drove, taking the short ride out to our family home on the south edge of town.

As we passed, I saw the new Mississippi and Missouri rail line station on what had been vacant ground three years previously. Our house seemed unchanged, or at least what I saw matched what I remembered.

While on leave, I was content to do nothing, or damn near it. Mom's plans for me centered on nightly dinners at our family table. Next came her measuring every seam to refit me with new cloth shirts, drawers and socks. Our Methodist church services were obligatory on Sundays. Visits from shirt-tail relatives, neighborhood friends and former schoolmates just happened, unscheduled, most afternoons or evenings.

The first shared obligation for Dan, Amos, and me was to visit the Evans family and express in person our admiration of their two sons. We spoke about their bravery but didn't say anything about their deaths, making our best effort at showing respect and honor, while sparing them needless pain.

Then we visited the Wenger family. Bill had been honorably discharged, having lost his left arm above the elbow. Back in town now, he was working as a handyman. I arranged for us to come back that evening.

The man we found was much changed from the Bill who'd stood beside me to enlist. He wore his empty left shirt sleeve tucked into his beltline. Quieter now and smiling less, he told us about his path from Shiloh home.

He'd not married, and his world seemed to have gotten smaller. Nothing out of West Union nor beyond the daily labor of his job.

"So how do you like the work?" I asked. "Do you get enough business?" His response seemed an attempt at humor, but darker, more ironic. Not what I recalled of my former cheerful friend.

"Hand down, I'm the best in town. If I can ever give either of your families a hand, just reach out." We all took turns shaking hands and exchanging promises to reunite in celebratory drinks after the Confederacy was defeated. Then the three of us went off for a nightcap before going our separate ways.

* * *

Dad was given leave from the Iowa Graybeards. We made a point of sharing a drink and a smoke every afternoon. It worked out that I was home for the stated monthly meeting of our Masonic Lodge. Dad and I attended together, he in his Sunday suit and me wearing my best suit, now awakened from its three-year rest in the closet of my bedroom.

My final day at home was full. Lots of goodbyes and a church auxiliary luncheon for West Union's three warriors about to return to the fray. I had little room to spare in my Gladstone bag, now stocked with socks, drawers and two blue cotton shirts. At our last family dinner, Dad handed me two bundles of cigars. "These should hold you for a while." From my mother, her final item was a packet of stationery paper and envelopes. Those came with her admonition, "Use them now."

April 25th was our non-negotiable departure date for the stage back to Davenport. We knew our destination: Cairo, Illinois, also on the Mississippi river but at the joining of Kentucky, Missouri and Illinois. What the future held in store, none of us knew, except that peace was neither in hand nor near.

I'd said goodbye to Mom at home, and Dad drove me to the station. We wished each other well, father to son and soldier to soldier. We three soldiers loaded our bags into the luggage boot of the coach. As I rode back to the waiting war, the prospect of the next battle hung heavy over my head.

12. On the Eve of Battle

Cairo, Illinois, Late April 1864

As we headed back, our small band increased as other Iowa men returning from their thirty days leave joined us. I was actually glad to see Sgt. Lakin and several of our officers.

"Finch, you smell like ten Mexican whores! You must have been on leave. So, tell me, son, are you ready to be a soldier like what we pay you for?" So came the greeting from Sgt. Lakin.

Our travel back was uneventful. No Confederates shot at our steamer as we made our way south along the winding Mississippi.

The upper Mississippi river is shallow. Many sandbars and islands sit amid the channels. Our lookouts did double duty, watching the channel for new sandbars as well as floating mines. The river flow doubled after the Missouri and Illinois rivers joined, just above St. Louis. We'd arrive in Cairo after three days travel.

When we got there, coal and food came aboard, but we were told not to get off. It fell to Major Crosley to enlighten us.

"We are continuing upstream. That big river joining the Mississippi over yonder is the Ohio. We are going to sail up the Ohio to Paducah, Kentucky. There we'll get on the Tennessee River and ride it to Clinton, Tennessee, where we will reunite with General Sherman's army. Enjoy the ride, because after that we'll be doing a lot of walking."

We started our march at Clinton on May 7th. Our regiment joined other Illinois and Ohio outfits until we were a full division, ten thousand strong. Now we began marching south. Eight days and one hundred seventy-five dusty miles later, we arrived in Kingston, Georgia. There we folded into Sherman's force: the Army of the Cumberland, Army of Ohio and us, part of General McPherson's the Army of Tennessee all together now. Our total force climbed to one hundred and ten thousand men.

Like Corinth and Vicksburg, Atlanta was vital to the rebels. Four railroad lines connected the city's industry with the rest of the rapidly shrinking Confederacy.

Always hot, our wool uniforms were soon sweat stained. Salt rings appeared under the armpits of my shirt and coat. The only change seemed to be that some days were both hot and wet from the rain. The ground, when not muddy, was uneven and hard with rocks which made themselves felt through the worn soles of my brogans. We marched with drummers tapping out a steady beat. Our singing sometimes competed or blended with other marching tunes. I knew that if the enemy didn't hear us, they would certainly smell us coming.

Flying and biting bugs became our constant companions. Only the smoke from our campfires provided any relief. We all scratched as we marched. I soon learned the easiest way to shift my musket from hand to hand. The itching from bites or sweat played no favorites with any portion of our bodies.

* * *

We arrived in Kingston on May 15th, and Atlanta was only sixty miles away. Now General Sherman reorganized his forces. Our regiment changed into an infantry battalion of three companies: A, B and C of the Iowa Second Veterans Infantry. With the reorganization came much-deserved promotions. I became a sergeant in Company B.

Feeling responsible for lives other than my own, I made a daily check on my men. Every ammunition and cap pouch had to be full. I taught them to smell their canteen water, checking that it was always safe. Not a simple speck of rust that could jam the hammer and trigger lock assembly was permitted in all of Company B.

Dan Daniels was also one of the company's sergeants. Our orders came directly from Lt. Col. Jacob Abernathy, a fine officer now in command of our small battalion. On July 8th, I got promoted again, this time from sergeant to lieutenant.

When time allowed, I cut and rolled small bandages. These and little bags of salt went to each of my men. Together in small groups, I explained to them how packing a wound with salt helps stop bleeding. The clean bandage could bind and our wood musket tompions plug a bullet hole. Our belts made tourniquets. All these field-expedient tricks might save their lives.

As we got closer to Atlanta, the Confederates began venturing out, probing our forces with small raids. They attacked us at Resaca and in late June at Kennesaw Mountain. They hit and ran, not wanting to stand and fight outside the well-prepared defenses that ringed Atlanta.

General Sherman had placed General McPherson's army on his left flank. When frontal attacks failed, the first plan became to cut off the rail supply lines. Our artillery would move up incrementally to better vantages from which to bombard the city's two concentric rings of defensive fortifications.

On July 20th, the Army of the Cumberland began what we hoped would be our final advance. McPherson's boys met the Confederates at Peach Tree Creek and fought them all day. They breached Union lines once, but we managed to push them back and force them from the field. It was a bloody day for us, but worse for the rebs. Seventeen hundred Union soldiers perished, with the Confederates leaving twenty-five hundred of their own dead on the field. Tomorrow was to be our Army of Tennessee's turn.

* * *

Being an officer in a small brigade gave me access to more information about battle plans, seldom explained to infantrymen. July 21st brought troop movements from both sides in preparation for their next attack.

General John Bell Hood had been given overall command of the Confederate forces. He had moved his forces out of the outer rings of Atlanta defenses. He wanted to take the strategic 'Bald Hill' position, now secured by Union artillery. A nighttime march just might surprise us with a sneak attack from our rear. But his troops were weary, their movements slow and not stealthy.

General McPherson moved all thirty-five thousand of the Army of Tennessee to an east-west line defending Bald Hill. This is where we found ourselves when dawn broke on July 22, 1864. In front of us stood forty thousand Confederates. But we held the high ground, and they had to attack into the fury of our guns.

Now Dan and I were the ones walking behind our infantry line. The bang and whizz of musket fire disappeared under the roar of our cannons, all dug in behind us on the crest of Bald Hill. The air was tinged gray by the musket smoke and stank from our sweat mixed with the sulfur of spent gunpowder.

We had been fighting for almost eight hours when a spot on the east end of our line broke. The rebs moved their attack, to force a break elsewhere under their overwhelming firing and with a bayonet charge. I heard the order from our captain.

"Company B, break left and fill the gap." That meant for us to do what had to be done. I searched in the smoke for Dan. We made eye contact and nodded our understanding. I gave the order to leave cover.

"Flank left, flank left… up and around…. move, move …. On my lead," and I stepped out front and waved us forward. We'd all go down together if it came to that, but we had to plug the hole in our line.

The shot that hit me was indistinguishable from all the noise of battle. It knocked me down, flat on my back. The sound and fury of the fight was no longer mine as I lay there, just one of many twisted bodies. My ears rang, but an unknown Union soldier was trying to get me up. His words drowned out the ringing in my ears.

"Leave me…leave me here, go." It was harder to say about myself than to give as an order. But it was the right thing to do. I hope I'd not lost my voice along with my hearing. He nodded and ran forward.

Lying wounded on the battlefield, I saw very little in front of me. After a while, I knew that I was alone on the field, alive among so many twisted, bloody dead. Now my body started to register pain. In those early minutes, all I knew was that my left shoulder had taken the hit.

But I couldn't move my left arm. Why or for how long, at that second, didn't matter. I fumbled to get to my haversack. I wanted salt and bandages for my wound, but they were beyond my reach. All my struggles did was speed me to pass out. At that moment, if I bled to death, I didn't care.

The last thing I remember from that bloody field was two gray-clad arms reaching under my shoulders and helping me to my feet.

13. Wounded and Captured

The Battle of Atlanta, July 22, 1864

It took me a while to sort things out in my mind. Why was I being captured and not killed? Our enemy had seldom been deliberately cruel, or at least not any more than we'd been. Two men carried me off the field, and the purpose in play came to me. Ah ha! My uniform showed me to be an officer. Union officers could be exchanged for their Confederate counterparts. Our trades were value for value, and not merely man for man.

I knew that until last year, battlefield exchanges of soldiers had happened. When the fighting stopped and, under the protection of a white flag, man for man exchanges of soldiers, those still fit for duty, took place. Infantry man for infantry man, sergeant for sergeant and officers of equivalent ranks also swapped one for one. Such trades came to an end when the Confederates would not send back black soldiers, and they had never resumed.

We were well into a pine wood when I saw the wagon up ahead. Sitting down flat in the bed were blue-clad wounded men. My two escorts helped me to the wagon and gave me a leg up. All of my weapons had been taken, but my haversack remained. I found myself sitting with seven other Union officers, all showing signs of wounds. What awaited us on the wagon was an unknown. Medical help or indifference to an enemy's suffering had yet to be revealed.

My left arm had been supported by one of the gray-clad guards who'd brought me to the wagon. Now it hung useless at my side. I felt every moment of the bullet wound. If my mind could separate bodily sensations, there was no pain coming from my arm, only my shoulder.

Our wagon ride, while hot and bumpy, was still preferable to walking. With the help of my neighbor in the wagon bed, I got the salt and bandages from my haversack. Struggling out of my uniform coat, I saw for the first time my bloody shirt. And then I saw the wound. A clean, round, black hole in my shoulder, underneath my collar bone, inches from my spine.

I pressed a palm full of salt into the oozing wound. The burning pain was terrible, and I struggled to keep from passing out. My hand needed to keep the salt in my wound to do any good, no matter the pain.

How far did we travel? Probably five bumpy miles to the interior of rebel lines. I didn't have the energy to turn or look ahead. Why bother? Finally, we reached a sizeable encampment of Confederate troops. When the wagon stopped, each of us was helped down and to our feet, if we could walk.

Those whose wounds left them immobile rode on stretchers and soon disappeared into what looked to be their hospital tent. I carried my shirt, jacket and haversack with my right hand, not wanting to lose control of anything that might soon make the difference between life and death. The rest of us, the walking wounded, went into a fenced enclosure to await our future.

When the gate to our holding pen swung open, it roused me back to full wakefulness. I saw a white cotton smock instead of a gray uniform. The orderly helped me to my feet and together we walked twenty feet into the lantern light of a hospital tent. I judged it to be a triage station, since there was no operating table or bloody refuse.

"Sit down," the orderly said and pointed to the sheet-covered table. I sat as directed. Beneath the table was a metal bucket of some sort. He took a seat on one of two camp stools that completed the furnishings in the tent. Soon a tall man, also in a bloodstained white smock, entered and stopped in front of me.

He didn't speak, nor did I. With practiced hands, he inspected my wound. "I see you did some first aid of your own, with the salt," and I nodded in confirmation. Then he asked, "Can you raise your arm?"

I answered, "No."

He lifted the arm from under my elbow.

"Does it hurt to raise your arm?"

And again, I answered "No."

Again he checked the wound and then lowered my arm. "The bleeding has subsided nicely. The lack of pain when I raised your arm tells me that the bullet, which is still in your shoulder, is not interfering with movement." Then, pulling over the other camp stool, he sat down in front of me.

"Lieutenant, you are a lucky man, notwithstanding being our prisoner. The bullet missed the axillary artery that feeds your arm. That's why you haven't bled to death. It also severed a network of nerves called the brachial plexus. They connect your shoulder to your spine. Your arm is paralyzed, probably forever." His manner was neither friendly nor hostile. I was a patient. He was a doctor and would act accordingly.

"My orderly is going to clean up and bandage the shoulder." He stood up and offered his right hand.

Then I noticed the square and compass on his ring, showing him to be a Master Mason. I took his hand in mine and, as taught, made the 'pass-grip' sign of recognition.

He recognized my unspoken message as I held the grip. His focus settled on me and my attention stayed on his face, neither of us speaking. Then, breaking eye contact, he gave directions to his orderly.

"I better clean and bandage the Lieutenant myself. This is a tricky wound. Bring a basin, antiseptic and bandages. I'll be all right here." And the orderly departed.

"Elijah Pitts, Acacia Lodge, Augusta, Georgia."

"Duane Finch, West Union Lodge, West Union, Iowa." We both fell silent when the tent flap opened and the orderly re-entered.

"I'll call when he's ready to go," and the orderly put down the supplies and exited.

"What happens to me now?" I asked.

Dr. Pitts answered as he cleaned and bandaged my shoulder. "You are all headed to Camp Sumter at Andersonville, Georgia."

Probably every Union soldier had heard stories about the horrors of Andersonville.

"That's bad," I said, and Pitts nodded. "I can keep you here for a few days because of your shoulder, but that is where all of you are going. I will do what I can to send a message to someone there who has also traveled and knows *the widow's son*."

His work was now completed. "I hope to sit in a lodge with you after the war." And with nothing more to be said, he stood and called for the orderly to come back. We shook hands once more before I was taken out. Escorted by a single guard, I joined other walking wounded in one of several guarded tents. There I remained for five days before being moved by wagon to Andersonville.

14. The Tortures of Camp Sumter

Andersonville, Georgia July 27 to November 20, 1864

As I rode along in the wagon of wounded officers, we were part of a parade of marching prisoners. Soon after leaving, we passed a small train station marked with the customary signage naming it, 'Lovejoy".

I knew Andersonville by reputation only, but not where it was. From the position of the sun, we were traveling south. As we moved along, the humidity increased, and we left behind the visible destruction that the war was inflicting upon the land.

I couldn't see the front or back of our parade of prisoners. They march us all night, with only occasional half-hour stops for water from passing springs. Some prisoners had rations in their haversacks; while most did not. Judging by the occasional flurry of shots that rang out, some prisoners tried to escape. How many made it? How many forfeited their lives, I didn't know.

We must have traveled fifty miles at least. By mid-morning on July 29th, the wood stockade wall came into view. I looked up as the first prisoners entered the stout wood gate at the wall rising a good eight feet above their head. Our wagon veered off to the right and moved along the perimeter to the back side of the prison. The medical tag provided by Doctor Pitts kept me out of the stockade.

National Park Reconstruction of Andersonville
Stockade

The camp medical unit was a collection of half a dozen rectangular tents. As we neared, there was a loose network of guard posts which kept an eye on the hospital. Since everyone there was wounded, they rightly judged our escape potential as pretty darn low.

Once our two wagons of wounded stopped outside the hospital tents, those of us who could walk were directed to a tent on the far right. Everyone else was taken by stretcher into one of the five other tents. Who among them went where? I didn't know.

I found myself among thirty or more Union soldiers with upper body wounds, like mine. There were head wounds, the blinded, the burned and even some amputees. Inside the visible insignias of rank were mostly missing, but I soon found that an organization of sorts existed.

"Soldiers of the Union army, I am Major Crocker and in charge of this medical tent," said the man with only one arm. We new arrivals watched and listened attentively.

"Outside this tent you are free to sit, write your letters or visit with your fellows. There is a low fence with Confederate sentries posted about ten yards beyond. The fence marks the bounds of our open access. Go beyond, you'll be sent back to the main stockade.

"Inside, you can take any empty bunk. Out back of our tent," and Crocker half-turned and pointed, "is our latrine." There is a daily

81

morning bed check at eight and again a nightly count at nine o'clock.

"Our rations are delivered twice a day. Eat it all. Expect an orderly to collect your medical tag." And he held up a rectangular tag, like the one tied to my coat. "The orderlies are prisoners like yourselves. Expect to see a doctor daily. He decides when you are well enough to move from here to there," and Crocker pointed out of the tent, towards the stockade. "Be polite to every guard, orderly and doctor, because they hold your life in their hands."

His welcome speech concluded, Major Crocker proceeded to meet us all individually. Where was home, what rank did we hold, our unit, and any news about the war's progress?

We chose our sleeping cots and shortly after surrendered our medical tags to an orderly. I began my own round of meeting tent mates. I met men from other Iowa units and others from Illinois and Ohio.

* * *

When the orderly entered the tent, everyone paused to listen and perhaps respond. "Finch!" I stood up immediately and raised my one good arm. At his two-finger gesture, I followed him outside into the Georgia sun. Down the row we went and entered the tent where bidden. Sitting at a folding camp desk was an older, white-coated man, tall and sporting a trimmed gray beard. I stood at his desk and waited silently.

With Dr. Pitt's tag in hand, he spoke a recognition challenge to me. "Hiram Finch," His mistake was deliberate. "I understand that you are a widow's son. Is that correct?" I answered the spoken challenge. "Sir, I've traveled a long way, from west to east. I'm not the widow's son, but I followed his designs at my work." My coded response was sufficient for the Confederate officer.

He stood and we shook hands. He was Glynne Lanier and belonged to an Atlanta lodge. "Let me have a look at your wound." While my arm remained useless at my side, the bullet wound was beginning to heal. He stepped back to his desk before speaking.

"Your arm is paralyzed for good, the nerves shot away. The bullet in your shoulder can stay, with no risk to you, if it causes you

82

no pain. I will check on you every other day, but when the wound is fully closed, I can't keep you here any longer. In the meantime, eat all you can, make as many friends as can, and write home.

"If things get too bad, listen for the bugle call at nine each morning for sick call and ask for me. I'll help if I can. Good luck." And with that, he sat down and called the orderly back inside.

For the next seven days, I took Dr. Lanier's advice. Our meals were usually cornbread, stewed greens seasoned with an occasional piece of bacon and what the Confederates claimed was coffee, but was actually chicory and parched wheat.

* * *

On August 5th, I passed through the rear gate of the stockade, to confront my new reality for however long it, or I, lasted. My eyes revealed part of the situation and my nose finished the job. Rotting, unwashed bodies, stinking open latrine pits and pools of water mixed into a putrid smell that hung over every surface.

Inside Andersonville, from NPS Archives

Flies swarmed about me. The very ground undulated with lice mixed into the dust. Where there was no dust, there was drying diarrhea, left where it fell by men too sick or weak to care or clean. Surely this was one of the inner rings of hell, but worse than Dante had imagined. The smell of decaying humanity hung thick in the air and seemed to stick to my skin. The collected smells could easily stink a bear off a gut wagon.

Three men approached me as I stood rooted to the spot, rendered unable to move by what waited ahead. The leader of the three saluted me and identified himself as the camp Chief of Police. He told me to come along with him to get settled. As we walked, he talked, and I listened. Perhaps to set my mind straight to realities of camp, he chose where to begin his narrative.

"I'm Sergeant Francis Muldoon, 54th Massachusetts Infantry. I'm going to escort you to an area where we have officers encamped."

In response, I identified myself by name, rank, and unit. Then it was time to listen and learn as the sergeant began telling me what I'd walked into. "There are over thirty-three thousand men in the stockade today.

"Here are the rules of Andersonville Prison. We used to have a problem with thugs robbing the weak. We hung them and don't abide any soldier victimizing a Union brother. I have the right to punish any man caught stealing. The punishment is cutting your rations in half and applying a number of lashes, not to exceed fifty." Turning to check my reaction, he asked if I understood.

I nodded.

"There are daily formations at 8 AM and 4 PM. Prisoners are divided into regiments of two hundred and seventy men and into ninety-man companies with a sergeant in charge. Your sergeant receives the rations and divides them up. Since the end of March, all we've gotten is cornmeal and salt. Sometimes it's cooked mush and sometimes a dry meal.

"If you have any money, there are peddlers from the town who come inside the stockade to sell food: wheat flour, vegetables and sometimes bones. They are robbers, but are your only option. If you are a religious fella, there are small ministries preaching on Sunday.

Others have prayer meeting or Bible reading somewhere in camp, most days. We even have two Catholic Priests who come in every Sunday."

As I followed him down through the compound, Muldoon and his deputies kept a watchful eye on what we passed and took care where they stepped. I understood why. His introduction continued, showing me that order was being attempted amid so much chaos.

He pointed out the nineteen-foot-wide space between the stockade wall and our shelters, and explained the meaning of "Deadline."

"You cross the line, and you are likely to be shot by one of the sentries in the guard towers."

"There is a post box. You can receive letters and packages and send letters that have been reviewed by the camp commander." I had yet to see any kind of barracks; all I could see inside the fifteen-foot-high stockade walls were ragged tents and lean-tos. Hundreds of hovels occupied every inch of available ground. There were gummed ground cloths, blankets, even overcoats used for shelter coverings. Then it hit me; our people had whatever they carried at capture, and nothing more.

The two slit-trench latrines we passed were permanently circled by swarms of black flies. When a ragged soldier took his turn to squat, his watery stool brought forth another swarm from inside the trench.

* * *

Finally, our small parade stopped near what I guessed was the south gate in the stockade wall. "Here we are, sir. Good luck," and with that, the three walked away.

Where the hell is here? No barracks, just more of the same lean-tos. Under the shade of their blankets or ground sheet covers, disheveled men huddled together for relief from the sun already beating down from above. I spied only hollow, vacant eyes as I looked from one unshaven face to another.

No one ventured out to greet me. I had never felt more alone than at that moment. So, I began to move between the hovels, looking for an unclaimed spot in the shade. Finding a place at last, I searched the group, then spoke before attempting to join. I pointed to the open space.

"Can I have that spot?" I got no reply, either through lethargy, indifference or loss of self. So I sat and hoped for the best.

Then the man next to me spoke. "Welcome to death's waiting room. Matthew Greely, 17th Ohio." He extended a dirty hand. I took it, happy for any recognition from one of the slumped men so near beside me. Greely's uniform was still whole and not yet reduced to rags. As he reached out to me, a visible crusting of salt and dirt cracked at his elbow.

"Duane Finch, Iowa 2nd Infantry." He nodded in response, so I continued. "How long have you been here?"

"Since May 17th; we got ambushed outside of Kingston. You?"

"July 22nd, at Atlanta."

He nodded and then asked if we'd taken Atlanta. I had to tell him no not yet. His chin dropped to his chest, perhaps at the loss of the faint hope that when we took Atlanta, as Sherman surely would, rescue would soon follow.

A faint hope seemed to be all Matthew Greely had to hang onto. The effect of my news on him was hard to watch. From my haversack, I took out my last two dry biscuits. A touch to his arm brought his head up and I passed one to him. We ate them in silence, together in what we had. And I felt better.

"Where do we get water?" I asked.

"Mostly we don't," came my neighbor's reply. As I stared back in silence, he explained what he hoped might save my life. "The stream is fouled. Don't drink it, ever. Some fellas dig holes for ground water but that's no better. The jackals…peddlers will be around later. Use any money you have, or trade goods, and buy clean water from one of them. We get rations most days and besides, it takes a lot longer to starve to death than to die of thirst."

Later, when the peddlers arrived, loudly hawking their wares, I bought a quart of water. It came inside a dried gourd and cost me a nickel and a promise to be a daily customer, negotiated down from two bits.

Alone with my thoughts in our silent blue sea, I realized I'd not written home since Kingston in mid-May. Back and forth swung my mind. Write and tell everyone I'm alive? Share the truth of my situation, or mercifully not share what hell looked like? In the end, I didn't write and passed the rest of the day sweating under the Georgia sun.

Hot as the day was, the night outside, unsheltered, was cold. But at least I had my uniform instead of the rags and tatters that I saw all around me.

* * *

The next day began when I shivered myself awake at first light. At the slit-trench latrine, I paid attention to where the edge of the trench had given away and dumped some poor soul into the filth.

At 8 AM I followed Matthew's lead and fell into our formation. After formation, everyone went back to queue up for whatever morning meal might arrive.

It was our own Iowa Sgt. Freitas who passed out the morning rations, a square of cold cornbread decorated with a stripe of molasses. The bread was dry as dust. Thankfully, my gourd still contained one last swallow.

We'd gone back to our shaded rest when the 9 AM trumpet sounded for sick call. Walking skeletons emerged from hovels all around me. As they struggled to form a line, an inmate wearing a white coat over his blue trousers questioned each man. Some men began to cry when he turned them away. Others simply turned and trudged back, now resigned to their fate.

While I was unable to overhear, my new friend Matthew explained. "If the orderly believes they are beyond hope, he sends them back. They only have two doctors to see the sick and not the hundreds that are dying." Soon after the men for sick call were led off, the trumpet blew again. "That's the call to bring out our dead," Greeley explained.

Perhaps my vacant place happened because, unknown to me yesterday, the south gate was where the dead were collected. From a hundred lean-tos bodies emerged, some carried, others dragged. They stacked them like cordwood parallel to the deadline. The gate opened and two wagons, each drawn by four mules, entered. With the wagon came gangs of Union prisoners to load the dead. Each crew member wore a ragged bandana over his nose and mouth.

But first, each body was stripped naked, and clothing now reduced to rags was thrown into a pile. The naked dead were then loaded into the wagons. Sometimes the skin on an ankle or arm was cloven from the flesh or the flesh from the bone. Finally, when the grim task was done, the wagons departed. I counted one hundred bodies.

When the gates closed, a swarm of scavengers descended on the pile of clothing stripped from the dead. Every scrap of cloth disappeared into their dirty hands to replace their own rags.

This scene was interrupted by another formation and feeding, and so ended my first full day inside Andersonville. The days just repeated themselves. On each of the next two mornings, I saw more than a hundred Union souls depart our little corner of hell.

15. Our Fates Change with the Wind

August 9th

All night on August 8th, heavy rain drenched us. The sounds of the stream that flowed through the camp foretold its ever-increasing volume. From a babble to a roar, the sound became difficult to ignore. While the men in our shelter slept, the stream did not rest.

The water escaped its confining banks as heavy rain and increased volume from upstream changed it to a flood inside the stockade walls. Awakened from the respite of sleep, those of us still strong enough snatched up and held onto anything we could. Everything else soon vanished in the flood. What little we had in clothing or shelter meant surviving another day, so we fought nature to save it all.

Then, with a crash, the waters tore through the stockade wall above its usual exit. The crash of the wall was barely audible over the rain and storm winds. I saw some prisoners bolt for the temporary opening, hoping to make a break for freedom. Some got through before the Confederates could mount a response. I watched as two cannons were rolled into the gap, one on each side of the rushing water. The attempts at escape stopped.

* * *

We waited in the rain, the skeleton of our tents and lean-tos scattered, but our coverings were held securely in a dozen hands. When the storm had run its course, I could see that the waters had cleansed the ground of our filth. And for a short time, the stream ran clear. From every corner of the camp, containers were being filled.

With the gift of clean water now in hand, Sgt. Muldoon posted trusted guards on a five-foot line along both sides of the stream. At all costs, the precious gift of clean water could not be squandered.

Three weeks later, on September 5th, prisoners heard the sentries talking about the fall of Atlanta on Sept 2nd. Perhaps Matthew's faint hope, rescue by our army, might come to pass. We heard that General Sherman's cavalry rode south, capturing a rail junction at

Macon and freeing Union prisoners at Camp Oglethorpe. Surely, they were on their way to Andersonville. The opiate of hope intoxicated us all. The Confederates certainly thought Andersonville would be an early target for Union cavalry, now free from battle.

On September 8th, the Confederates marched eight thousand able-bodied prisoners out of Andersonville. According to our guards, they were going to camps further east in Georgia. By the end of September, all of our thirty thousand were gone except twenty-five hundred who were either too sick, weak or were needed for operating the camp. Now, I faced a choice, and the ending of either path was an unknown. Should I go to another camp, perhaps better, but maybe not? Or should I volunteer to remain here?

Even with only one good arm, I could swing a hammer and was willing to work on the construction of barracks. Things began to change. Our rations increased and loads of lumber began to arrive. Andersonville was to become a prison hospital. By October, new prisoners stopped arriving, but the daily death count remained high. Only the sickest had been left behind.

As the days turned to weeks, Matthew Greeley and I continued to work side by side, building barracks. Escapes became routine as rebel guards disappeared, transferred or deserted. We didn't know how, but they were gone, none the less.

Finally, on November 20th, we were offered parole. We both signed the parole documents, promising not to take up arms again during the war. We were let through the south gate, my useless arm thrown over Matthew's shoulder. Like two schoolgirls, we skipped and sang a ragged chorus of "When Johnny Comes Marching Home."

16. Free at Last!

November 1864

We met our first Union cavalry less than two miles outside the stockade gate. What a pitiful sight we must have been. The sergeant leading the patrol dismounted and helped each of us up to ride behind one of his troopers.

That night, I ate hot food, served with real coffee. My dirty uniform was exchanged for new and hot water was provided for a long overdue bodily cleaning. Word of our arrival went to the Army of Tennessee's command. My new friend for life, Matthew Greely, received thirty days' leave.

A Union doctor I saw in Georgia hoped that the use of my arm could be restored, and the army was going to try to do that for me. He also told me I was one of the lucky ones to have survived, because nearly 13,000 of us died there from disease, poor sanitation, malnutrition, overcrowding, or exposure.

The Union doctors agreed with the diagnosis of Doctor Pitts. My arm was lost to me, its nerves irreparably severed, unless the bullet still in my arm was just impinging on the nerve. Could removing the bullet return the function to my arm? No one knew, but I asked them to try. I had nothing to lose. I joined a convoy of wounded headed north to the naval Academy at Annapolis, Maryland. The hospital there was the best the Union had to offer. Perhaps a simple surgery might restore the use of my arm, and a surgery was scheduled.

With the ether, I felt nothing until after surgery, but then I was in pain for days. Laudanum helped and allowed me to sleep, but it stopped me up something fierce. I feared I would never take a good dump again. But finally, this too came to pass. The surgery removed the Confederate Minié ball, but it didn't restore use of my arm.

Our ward was run by Nurse Emily Dana. All of her charges were survivors of the camps at Andersonville, Belle Island, or Libby Prisons. Nurse Dana was our sunbeam and no one on the ward ever complained. Death still took many from their wounds and the complications of starvation.

Since my capture, I'd decided not to write home. My circumstance, if known, I thought would be worse for my folks than not knowing. Free at last and with my injury confirmed as irreparable, I could at last write with accuracy about my situation.

In less time than ever before, I got a letter in return. To them I was back from the dead, as I was reported killed at Atlanta. My obituary had appeared in the local paper and a memorial service had taken place at our church.

17. The Dawn Before the Darkness

Nurse Dana stood over me, arms akimbo. "Lt. Finch, We need your bedspace. It's time for you to move on. Go see Warren, our ward clerk, and tell him to transfer you to the medical holding company. Take your shaving kit and toiletries with you. Good luck to you now." She smiled and pivoted back to her duties.

I had been in a gray nightshirt, blue wool robe, and slippers since arriving. So, I left the multi-bed ward and approached Warren, who was busy at his desk. I knocked before entering.

"Yes," he said, looking up from his papers. He pushed his iron-rimmed glasses up the bridge of his nose with an index finger, paused and waited. Warren was a soldier, judging from the uniform coat hanging on a corner coat rack.

"I'm being moved to a medical holding company."

"Name?" His glasses slipped down the bridge of his nose as his focus shifted to a tray of folders. Locating mine, he opened the brown cover and made an entry on the topmost page. "Take this down the hall to the Quartermaster for your uniform issue." He never looked up but closed the folder and passed it across the desk to me.

"Thank you," I replied. *Damned headquarters weasel. Give 'em hell, Warren.* The folder contained my medical records beneath a cover sheet pertaining to my change in status from patient to soldier in a holding company.

* * *

I found the quartermaster's door at the end of the same long hallway. Entering, I faced a long counter, behind which towered a wall of high wooden shelves packed with bins of clothing. A private standing behind the counter motioned me forward. "Folder please, sir." My nightshirt and robe identified me as a recovered patient.

From beneath the counter, he retrieved a medium-sized wicker basket and passed it to me. This time, as an officer now, my issue included two sets of light-weight wool long johns, wool socks, my belt with the officer's buckle, and black leather boots.

"Waist size, sir?" Hearing 32 inches, he turned, located the bin marked 'wool pants 32.' He removed two pairs and placed them in the basket. We moved slowly down the line as he asked, and I answered, about each garment I was entitled to receive. "What size Kepi cap, sir?"

"Medium, I suppose?" I said.

The clerk nodded and passed me a cap. "Try this one."

It fit. I took it off and put it on top of the other items in the basket.

The final question was about emblems of rank. "Shoulder boards, sir?"

No one on the line wore shoulder boards, as they served only to mark us as targets. "No, just collar brass. Thanks."

"All right, sir, that completes the issue. If anything doesn't fit, bring it back and I'll trade it out for another, sir." He pointed me down the hall to my next station stop, the property room

I waited at the counter until the clerk emerged from a shelf-lined aisle. I handed him the brown folder, and he began thumbing through a wooden box of index cards. Finding mine, he looked over and asked, "No property, sir?"

"Nothing that I want as souvenirs from Andersonville."

He responded with a nod, then initialed and passed back my folder. "Through the door on your right, sir. Cashier's next."

My pay was $105 per month since my release, and $1 per day for my one hundred-seventeen days as a prisoner. I was handed $432, which was the most money I'd ever had at one time.

Through the next door, and I was in a large common area. Men in uniform sat alone or in groups, some playing cards. A sign showed "Medical Holding" above the double doors on the right. Doors on the left were marked, "Dining Hall." And between those two, half-glass doors showed hospital grounds beyond. I knew to look for the ward clerk so I could check in and be assigned a bed and locker.

Beneath the 'Medical Holding Company' sign was a small office. Inside sat a soldier in uniform. The stripes on his sleeve also had a diamond tucked inside the chevrons. I was now in an active-duty company, so there was no clerk, instead a First Sergeant, who kept the personnel records and maintained discipline in the company area.

I set my wicker basket down and knocked on the office door frame, even though as an officer I outranked him. Military courtesy. He looked up from his work. "Come."

I handed him my folder and waited silently while he perused its contents. After a minute, he pointed to the wooden chair facing his desk. "Please take a seat, Lieutenant."

"Welcome to the company, sir. I'm First Sergeant White. Did the doctors do you any good, sir?"

"No, but I appreciated their efforts."

"So, let me explain how this unit works."

I sat and gave him my attention.

"I'll get you a bed and locker in the officers' section. Reveille sounds at 0600 and Retreat at 1800. Your bed must be made, and we have a morning inspection daily at 0800 and a formation at 1830. Our dining hall is for all ranks and meals are: 0700, 1200 and 1900 daily. You no longer eat for free. Officers pay twenty-five cents per meal, and you can pay in advance or monthly. I have a company safe here in my office, if you want me to secure your pay or any personal possessions."

I passed him my $432. "Please deduct one week's worth of meals for now and let me know when I owe more."

He nodded. "You've seen the day room and the grounds beyond. They are available to everyone. If you need to go on sick call, tell me at Inspection." With his list of rules now explained, he concluded and rose from his seat. "So, follow me, sir, and I'll find you a bed."

1st Sgt. White moved ahead of me, and we left his office. I followed him down the center aisle of a large open-bay barracks, and past a multi-man latrine.

We passed through double doors and into another barracks area. This had two-man rooms off a central hall with a latrine off to the right side. At the second room on the left, 1st Sgt. White gestured to the iron-framed bed on the left. An open clothes closet and two drawers were built into the wall. The window looked out towards a parade ground.

"Your roommate is Capt. Alonzo Belnap. I'll leave you to get settled in and change into uniform. Stop by my office when you're dressed and I'll introduce you to Capt. Belnap, if he hasn't found you already." The orientation concluded, 1st Sgt. White walked out.

I began to unload my basket, hanging or folding items as I went. *Well, there is more privacy than on the ward, so that's good.*

First, I climbed into my new drawers. No problem there, until it came to the eight buttons running from neck to crotch. Slowly, I managed to tip each button into the buttonhole and then try to hold it with my thumb and push it into the hole. Four times I tried this, before one button was secured. *Shit!* I would save the issue of the drop seat buttons for another day.

Now for my uniform shirt and its seven buttons. *God damn it!* Finally, in frustration, I satisfied myself with only buttoning every other button and ignoring the bottom two that would be inside my trousers. It had to get better with practice.

Now it was time for my trousers and their button at the waist and the three-button fly. With the cloth fly covering the buttons, I couldn't use the tedious method that worked on my shirt and drawers. "Damn it," and I kicked out, forgetting my feet were in slippers, not brogans. My frustration had turned to anger and now the anger became pain. I cursed in more than a normal volume as my frustration grew.

I dropped down onto the iron bunk and massaged my wounded toes. It didn't help. Leaning my chin in my palm, I just wanted a respite from the frustrations of being a one-armed man.

Back at Andersonville, where no one bathed and everyone stank, my drawers stayed unbuttoned and my brogans untied. Details such as these hadn't mattered when life was a day-to-day thing.

Probably ten minutes passed as I sat there with my throbbing foot and unfocused mind. Finally, when I could think of no other way, I pulled on my robe and slippers. Back at the sergeant's office, I knocked, my two pairs of trousers in hand, and waited for White's eyes to meet mine.

"My uniform trousers are too small. I need to go back to the clothing issue." White nodded but didn't speak. "Is there a way to get back there without going through finance and property stations?" There was, which the sergeant proceeded to show me.

The same clerk was on duty.

"Hello, again. I need bigger pants: 34s please," and I put the 32s up on his counter. He gave them a refold and exchanged them for 34s.

"Would you button the fly buttons for me, please?" The request brought a quizzical look, but he complied. I thanked the young soldier, shook his hand, and walked back to my quarters. I sat down on the iron framed bunk and, securing one boot heel with the other boot, took my footgear off. My unspoken mantra was, *please work, please work, please work.*

When I stepped into one pair of trousers, a loud "Yes," escaped my lips, and I breathed a deep sigh of relief. My belt would keep the oversized pants from falling down. With this problem solved, I had much to strategize over, but I needed a rest from dealing with the newly realized issues of my new, one-armed life.

At the rate I was going, if I get up at 0500, I can be dressed by breakfast. What a piss poor prospect!

Sighing, I returned to the common area. "Sgt. White, I'm ready to meet Capt. Belnap."

"Yes, sir." He got up, and together we walked across the common area. "The noon meal is being served. Let's check in the dining hall."

I followed him in. The hall was filled with four-man tables, with a food service counter on one side and a beverage counter with a coffee urn and ceramic water pitchers on another.

"That's Capt. Belnap, at the table on the far right." White pointed as he spoke. "Enjoy your meal, sir," he said and turned and left.

Belnap was sitting alone, so I went to pick up my meal.

I watched him as I moved through the line. I held my tray out for each item I wanted on my plate. Then I saw the entrees. *Shit, those steaks look good, but I better not.* I could either hold the steak on my fork and eat as a giant meatsicle, or ask someone else to cut it for me. *Mommy, will you cut my meat?* I didn't want the dinner in my lap because I tried to cut it myself. "Meat loaf, please," and I walked to Belnap's table.

Another soldier placed a plate of food in front of the captain. *Humm, service from a junior officer? Maybe no legs? Paralyzed? What?*

"What have I got?" Belnap asked the unknown server.

"You've got corn bread at twelve o'clock, succotash at four, meat loaf with gravy at seven, and boiled potatoes at ten." The server took a seat on the captain's immediate right as Belnap slowly reached out for a tin cup, six inches behind the plate. His table mate moved the cup slightly to meet the grasping hand.

Belnap is blind. "Gentlemen, may I join you?"

Both men looked up from their plates, but it was Capt. Belnap who spoke. I studied his face. His eyes were neither closed nor sunken. In fact, they were open and seemed to be looking directly back at me. "Please join us." Both men laid down their forks and reached out to me in an exchange of greetings.

"Phineas Fitzgerald."

"Lon Belnap,"

"Lt. Duane Finch, Capt. Belnap's new roommate." I'd stick to proper military courtesy for one, maybe two superior officers, until they said otherwise.

"Welcome, Duane, don't worry about all the niceties. First names are fine with us," said Belnap.

I appreciated their attitude. The medical holding company, at least for these men, was not about ranks or salutes. The bond between the two was apparent.

"Finn here is waiting for surgical," said Belnap.

"Well, good luck Finn," I said. "What are they doing?"

Again, the response came from Belnap. "Penis reduction surgery," he said with a straight face. "For the second time. Finn here is hung like a horse, but his wife has suffered enough. Now he'll probably be hung like a hamster." It took me just long enough to recognize the joke that they both snickered before I smiled my appreciation.

"He's mustering out tomorrow," corrected Belnap.

"So, what about you, Duane?" inquired Finn. "Are they going to fix your arm?"

I shook my head and explained that the doctors had tried and failed, so I was awaiting a medical board review for a disability rating, and then mustering out.

"What's wrong with your arm?" Belnap asked. "It looks fine to me," and both my new friends laughed again.

"It's paralyzed. A bullet to the shoulder severed the nerves." I decided it was a good time to begin eating.

As our meal neared its end, I offered to bus our dishes. Finn announced that he had an appointment, and he rose from the chair. A squeak betrayed the hinges of a wooden leg, even before it showed in his movement.

"Oil, thy self, Squeaky," kidded Belnap. "He's going to get fitted with a new pair of shoes. I call him Fearless Fitzgerald, because he doesn't know the meaning of fear. Terror, yes. The only things he fears are beavers and termites." We shook hands as he departed.

"Lon, after I get rid of the dishes, I'm going outside for a smoke. Can I help you with anything? Getting back to the room? Join me for a smoke?"

"Duane, do you have a watch? I have a meeting with one of my doctors at one." He paused for a moment, then with the same straight face, spoke. "I forgot mine."

When I told him it was 12:30, he asked if I'd bring him a refill on his coffee. I cleared the table and brought us each a second cup. Lon Belnap couldn't see the smile that his sense of humor brought out in me. I would take care not to assume him incapable of anything, especially since I couldn't even manage buttons.

* * *

As we sat with an extra cup of coffee and too much time to fill, our conversation was respectful but very open. I answered his questions about my background, friends lost, and the Andersonville experience. Then, I asked about his eyes.

"They don't know what's wrong. Some of the doctors are convinced I'm malingering. But there are others who see me as crazy or suffering from something called 'Conversion Hysteria' or 'Hysteric blindness.' Remember, these are the smartest people in this man's army; just ask 'em."

"So, are you crazy?" I asked.

"Who knows? The army's problem is I fought through enough battles that malingering doesn't seem to fit. It happened at Gettysburg, during Pickett's Charge. I watched Confederate General Armistead shot down, and then only darkness."

99

"But if it makes you feel any better, I don't play with my shit and I don't think I'm a woman trapped in the body of a man. So, you have nothing to fear."

"Well, that's a relief."

"I'm glad that at least one of us is feeling better. If they decide I'm crazy, then I'm off to the St. Elizabeth Hospital, the army's nut house over on the Anacostia outside the Capitol. If they decide I'm malingering, then it's a dishonorable discharge, loss of rank and disability pay."

"So, what are they doing now?"

"Well, some days doctors look into my eyes trying to diagnose my blindness. Other days, different doctors mostly test me to see if I'm faking."

"How?"

"Once they let me step on a rake. If I could see, I wouldn't. But I couldn't see it and got hit right in the face. Sometimes they put things in my path to see if I'll forget and avoid the trap. I never do and have the bruises to prove it."

"Bastards."

"Another time they pretended they were going to stick a knife in my face. And when I didn't flinch or grab their hand, it pissed them off. Otherwise, I would probably never have known."

Hearing the alternate futures Belnap faced caused us both to pause. With our cups empty, he asked for help to the latrine. Leaving him at the door, I walked outside for a smoke and to quietly practice on buttons.

My problems don't amount to a pinch of shit compared to his.

18. Beginning a New Life

1865-1866

The pension board in Washington created a scale for disability pensions. How much was an arm worth? A leg? Both legs or both arms? It was all there in black and white. One arm or leg went for $15 per month. So did a hand or foot. But both hands, arms or legs were worth a tidy $25. The only real deal was loss of one eye. That netted you $25 a month and you got to keep the other eye.

Anyway, in March, 1866, I began receiving a disability payment of $15 and I was mustered out of the army. Since the average monthly income nationwide was about $42, my $15 gave me a good start.

My roommate was still a curiosity for the doctors, to be tested or tricked. Well, at least until his novelty wore off, and they decided what to do with him. My hope was that he'd be granted a disability pension and mustered out.

* * *

I left the hospital two months after my arrival and was sent to a medical holding company in Jeffersonville, Indiana. It was there that I mustered out, across the Ohio river at Louisville, Kentucky, on July 12, 1865. I was given a rail and river voucher to allow me to travel home.

Since 1862, President Lincoln had made it the law that veterans would be compensated for their service for as long as they lived. So too, our wives and widows would never go without, thanks to husbands that had answered his call.

* * *

My route home by rail went first through Pittsburg, then Ft. Wayne and Des Moines. I had to change trains in Pittsburg. During the lay-over, my Gladstone bag went into a locker at the station, and I walked the city's downtown. I traveled in my uniform, as buying new clothes seemed less important that getting home.

"Have you got a light for a lady?" a soft voice asked.

I'd been happily enjoying my cigar and looking at the storefronts and buildings along the way. When I stopped and turned my head towards the voice, I saw the speaker. She stood under a light post at the curb on my right.

"Are you looking for some company, Soldier?" She was young and attractive. The streetlight showed her hair as bright copper. Her long dress and short jacket were of deep red velvet and a matching hat topped her head.

"How about that light?" and she held out an unlit cigarette. I understood her offer, as it was not the first I'd ever received. And I was interested. I dug a wooden match from my pocket, turned to face her and struck the match on the metal lamp post.

My eyes stayed on her as I lit her cigarette.

Her eyes appraised me before anything more was said. I expected an offer, but no. "Sorry, no offense, but I don't do gimps."

I said nothing as things began to sink, including my eyes. I dropped the match and started back towards the train station.

* * *

I made it home on August 8th, 1865. A rail connection now passed through West Union. My first ever train ride was every bit as noisy as any coach trip, but considerably less bumpy.

Dad had been discharged from the Graybeards. My first questions for him were about the fate of my comrades Dan and Amos? Dad told me. Amos died in the battle of Savannah in December 1864. His sacrifice had been part of the price paid by the Army of Tennessee as they marched with General Sherman to the sea. At least the taking of Savannah brought the March to the Sea to a successful conclusion. I'm not sure if Amos would have considered the campaign successful.

Dan Daniels had survived and was home now, back working at the library and soon to be a father again. I put seeing Dan at the top of my "to do" list. But not yet. So many things to do: reconnecting with friends, Bill Wenger, Masonic lodge brothers and church congregants. But not yet.

"Dad, I'm tired from the trip and I need to go to bed."

With the window shade pulled down and the door shut, I spent my next two days in the dark. I did my best to clear my mind, to not think at all. When I did think, the same thoughts came again and again. I was sinking into the deep blue-black of nothingness.

You can't write, you can't cut a steak, you can't tie your shoes, you can't button your clothes. You're a gimp. No woman will ever want you.

At the bottom of the dark place lay my understanding about how to end the pain and the problems. How to not be a gimp. The thought of peace being within reach was seductive.

Two days after I went to bed, my slumber was interrupted. The dark behind my eyelids could tell when the bedroom blinds went up. Somewhere out there, my father's voice. "Time to get up." When I didn't move, he ripped the cover off me. I still did nothing and was glad when he gave up and left.

* * *

"Rise and shine, baby brother." The voice was my brother Burns. I cracked one eye open from my pillow. Clem, my other brother, stood at the foot of my bed. The two of them proceeded to pick me up and carry me through the house to the front porch. And drop me.

My head banged the wood floor as did my right elbow, and I began to howl in pain. I lay there crumpled on the porch, cursing the two of them. The only thing that didn't hurt was my left arm.

"Well, he's alive," said Burns.

"Are you sure? He smells dead," quipped Clem.

My eyes were open now, and I was mad, no longer lost in my own head. My brothers were looking down on me from above.

"You're right, he does stink."

Burns toed me with his boot. "Duane, you smell like the Devil's asshole. We don't want you stinking up our mother's house." Then they sat down on the porch swing and left me on the floor.

I winced as I sat up and then managed to rise to my knees and finally stand. I stood silent and faced the two, who returned my stare from their seats on the swing.

Finally, Clem spoke. "We will help you with whatever you need, however we can. But not with what you're doing now." He paused, but his eyes never left my face.

I moved to the porch rail opposite the swing and faced the two. My anger had passed.

"Tell us the problems," said Burns.

I began listing my problems: writing, dressing, eating and feeling that I was less of a man that I'd been before.

They listened. Neither dismissed anything I'd said. Instead, each offered suggestions, some obvious to them, if not to me.

"Boots."

"Practice writing. It will get better."

"Ask them for smaller pieces of meat. Eat more chicken legs."

"Some woman will look beyond the arm if you pay more attention to her than you do to yourself."

We'd become brothers again, never easy but always caring. And when Burns directed me to "go take a bath," I did.

* * *

When I went to get dressed two days later, I found my garments changed: mother's adaptions of my clothes to fit my circumstances.

Underwear was now two pieces, not one, and the bottoms had a single button at the waist and no buttons on the fly flap. The upper part was altered so that all but the top three buttons were gone. There were bigger buttonholes, and the placket was stitched shut. Trousers I'd left at home now had suspenders attached to buttons on the sides and back of the waistline. I could pull the pants on and slide under the suspender straps.

Her love had manifested in simple adjustments that eased my self-doubts and fears. I felt ready to reconnect with the world.

* * *

When I arrived at their front door, Ida Daniels greeted me with a one-armed hug, all that her pregnancy permitted. I came Sunday afternoon, well past any church service. I wanted to see my friend together with his growing family at their home, and not to intrude on his work time at the library.

A small boy peeked around his mother's skirt and stared up at me. He was an infant when my five friends and I went to war, and only three when Dan and I came home on leave. I was still an unknown person to him, so he hung back.

I went down on one knee, and young Samuel, taking cues from his mother, finally ventured out. My extended hand garnered a smile and a small hand to shake.

"Duane, welcome back. Get in here." She kept an arm around my waist, then turned and called to her husband. "Daniel, Duane's here," and she guided me into the house. The bright sun flooded the parlor with light. Ida kept a neat house. No dust floated in the beams streaming in.

She ushered me to a button-tufted chair upholstered in deep red. A rich, inviting background note of pipe tobacco filled the room. I stood, waiting for her to seat herself in the other upright chair. Instead, Ida Daniels remained standing. *Too pregnant to sit?*

My question was soon answered when Dan walked in.

"Samuel and I are going to leave you two men to your catching up." Then, with a big smile, Ida left the parlor, retreating down the same hall from which Dan had emerged.

Then I reached out to shake hands with this dear man with whom I'd shared so much. He clasped my forearm with his right and put his left arm around my shoulders. No words passed between us for a long moment. "Did your folks tell you we heard you died in the battle and your body was lost?"

"Yes, Dad told me."

Then with a pat to my shoulder, he pointed me to one of the two red-upholstered chairs that bracketed a small table. I took the chair on the right, so my good arm was available. Now I notice the metal humidor, six-pipe rack and ashtray on the tabletop.

I told him what I remembered from July 22, when I was shot. About Andersonville, and Matthew Greeley and the other friends who'd guided and helped me survive, when so many others had not.

And the help I received through Masonic fraternity and charity. Finally, I spoke about the hopes of the Union doctors at Annapolis, sadly unrealized.

Newspaper stories prompted first one question and then another from Dan. Did I know what had happened to BG Lauman after Atlanta? Did I know what happened to Confederate Capt. Henry Wirz, the commandant of Andersonville? I knew neither, so he told me the rest of their stories.

"Lauman was a hero at Fort Donelson and Hatchie Bridge, but he made enemies along the way, including General Ord. After Jackson, General Sherman chose to believe his Corps Commander, General Ord, over the explanation of a subordinate Division Commander. Lauman was relieved of command and sent home to Burlington, Iowa, to await orders.

"According to the Washington papers, Wirz had met his end. Captain Henry Wirz, the Andersonville stockade commander, was arrested and charged with 'murder, in violation of the laws of war.' Tried and found guilty by a military tribunal, Wirz is to be hanged on November 10, 1865. He was the only Confederate officer charged or convicted of a war crime. Somebody needed to pay."

Silence filled the room after Dan's revelations. I didn't want the visit to end, but we both needed a pause, a full stop in the conversation. So, I spoke up. "Dan, how about we have a smoke? I see a pipe."

"That's a great idea. I'm guessing you've got one of those nasty, skinny cigars somewhere inside your coat?

I chuckled and reached into the left inside pocket of my coat. Out came one of my favorite cigars. I held it horizontally and passed it slowly below my nose, deliberately making a show of savoring its aroma.

We were both smiling now. Dan chose a pipe from among his collection. He opened the table-top humidor and loaded rough-cut tobacco into its bowl. Then he paused to tamp down what was already loaded before finishing filling the pipe and giving it another tamp with his right thumb.

"Ida would want us to take our smoking outside."

I nodded my understanding.

"Come on, we'll go out on the front porch." I followed his lead as he rose, grabbing a wad of wooden matches from their holder in the center of his ashtray.

Outside on the covered porch, he pointed to their glider swing and motioned for me to sit. I chose the left corner seat and we both sat. Dan struck a match on the wooden arm rest. He leaned over, offering the flame first to me. Leaning in to get a good light, I sucked in the first few puffs of smoke, and then watched as he worked on lighting his pipe.

"You two-armed guys have it easy, lighting up."

My comment made Dan smile, and after his first few puffs of smoke, he replied. "Well, next time, try to get shot in the leg, or the ass."

We talked about friends we'd known. Who didn't make it back? Who did, but at what price? Our conversation slowed, as we were both comfortable in a shared silence.

Dan's pipe smoke came now in smaller puffs. My cigar had dwindled in length by half, so I could clench it in my side teeth and talk. With my one good hand, I reached over and grabbed his left wrist before speaking, slowly, deliberately now. Dan turned his head in my direction but remained comfortable just listening.

"I'm a lot smarter now than I was when we all placed our hands on the flag in Sheriff McPherson's office. When I think about you, and Matthew, Amos, Bill and all the other friends I've had, it was friends that got me through the war. The songs we shared around our campfires. Ida's letters and their news from home. The kinship I felt from the other soldiers, all unknown to me, except that they were there fighting at my side."

He slid his arm around until he held my hand in his. We sat in silence, with only an occasional bird song or small metallic squeaks of the glider swing as background. Our silence seemed to fit my moment of personal revelation.

I suspected I could sit there on Dan's porch for as long as I wanted, or perhaps needed. As the sun began to sink toward the horizon, it was time for me to go. "I'd best let you get back to your pretty wife and Sam. I'm expected back for Sunday dinner and there's hell to pay if I'm late." I reached down to steady the glider seat with my right hand and got to my feet.

Standing beside my comrade, I asked him to say goodbye to Ida. "Let's meet again soon and talk about what I'm doing here in West Union, now that I'm recovered and rested. I want to do something more. And besides, the town already has a one-armed handy man."

"Sure, we can. You stop by the library anytime and we'll get it going." We shook hands and as I began to step off the porch, I heard Dan's final goodbye over my shoulder. "Those cigars of yours still smell like you're smoking a turd."

* * *

Bill Wenger still lived in the same place where Dan, Amos, and I had found him. I located him in his small kitchen. He greeted me with a broad smile before turning on his dark wit.

"Couldn't you at least have arranged to get shot in the other arm? We could have been great Siamese card playing twins, if we mastered a two-hand shuffle. Now you're no damn good as a card partner."

"Well, it's nice to see you too, Bill." I reached out and took his hand, pulling him close.

"I'd give you a pat on the back, but my left my arm is in my other shirt. Sorry," he said in a practiced tone that fit the absurdity of our situation. "Come on, sit down and I'll pour us a drink." I sat and Bill retrieved two shot glasses that he pinioned together with his thumb and forefinger. I watched my friend and noted all the little ways that, over the months, he'd adapted to deal with his limitations.

"I got back three weeks ago and I'm glad to see that you are your same sweet, agreeable self." While I spoke, Bill set a bottle down on the tabletop and wiggled the cork free, then poured whiskey. We clicked glasses and drank down the amber liquid.

I spoke about Andersonville, the flood and Matthew Greeley. Then I told about the hospital and Lon Belnap. Nothing needed to be said about Atlanta or my wound. Bill had lived the experience, so there was no more to say.

I took a refill when he offered, and the conversation moved on to what comes next. "Well, the one-armed handyman position is already filled. Sorry. I can get you a job as an apprentice paper

108

hanger. And I hear the cat house over on third Street is in need of a piano player."

"Jeez, thanks Bill; and I thought it was going to be tough to find a job." With two drinks in me, I needed to stop. I thanked my friend and assured him we'd stay in touch for as long as I stayed in West Union.

19. What Comes Next?

1866

I wanted to be occupied. The war had left me with a taste for being part of something. Long and short of it, finding work I liked was now necessary. I'd waited enough already in life: at army camps and as a hospital patient. Then there was my longest forced wait, wondering when it would be my turn to be dragged out at the morning bugle call to a last wagon ride.

Somewhere along the line, I'd lost my fear of dying. But what scared me now was wasting time. Time is the only thing in life we can't replace or acquire. Christmas had passed three months ago. I'd pissed away enough of my life. It was time to get moving, to where or what I wasn't yet sure. But moving none the less.

* * *

We were having an afternoon smoke outside on the front porch. "Dad, I need to be moving along. It's time." Dad said nothing and didn't ask me why. His briar pipe, filled with fine rubbed burley tobacco, burned without expelling smoke. Only the small puffs that he occasionally exhaled confirmed the bowl was lit.

Did he not hear me?

At long last, he removed the pipe from his mouth. Pulling a small metal tool from his shirt, he began tamping down the burning tobacco. I was about to repeat myself when he looked up from his pipe and focused on me. "I understand; been there myself, as a young fella."

I knocked off an inch of white cigar ash with a swat of my index finger, returned the cigar to my mouth and withdrew a clipping from my shirt pocket. "Take a look at this," and I passed it over. Dad put the pipe stem back in his mouth and cradled the paper in his hand, his eyes moving across the 'help wanted ad.'

I knew the copy by heart. Since my first reading in a random newspaper, as I waited in the local barber shop.

Wanted

Single men: orphans and veterans preferred.
Barlow and Sanderson Stage line is hiring drivers, guards,
station managers and stockmen for our western expansion.
Contact Bradley Barlow, Courtland Hotel, Kansas City, KS.

"Son, you volunteered to fight for the Union. You can do any damn thing you want. You are a better man with one arm than most fellas are with two. Your pension guarantees you'll never go hungry," and he went back to tending his pipe.

"When do you plan to head out?" My Dad was a man of few words. His response suggested both approval of my choice and more importantly, confidence in me. My having only one arm didn't matter. Each new problem was solvable, one at a time.

"In two days' time. I've got a few goodbyes to say."

That garnered another nod. "Your mother will want to have the news come from you," and that got him my nod in return.

Dad took his pipe from his mouth. Rising from his seat, he tapped the bowl clean of white tobacco ash at the edge of the porch. "We need to have a drink, son. This is a big thing for any fella, starting a new life chapter."

"Do you want me to hitch up the mule, and we go into the bar at the Howard?" I asked.

"Nah, your mother knows I take a drink from time to time. Hell, she'll even have a drink herself once in a while. If you are fine with rye whiskey, I'll bring out my bottle."

I snuffed out my cigar butt and pocketed the stub. "Fine."

Dad turned to go back inside. Then at the door he inquired, "Do you take it neat or with a water back?"

"I don't like it watered down. Straight up and neat." I leaned back and waited. The air was cooling from the first warm days of April. The flying bugs that appeared on every warm Iowa afternoon hadn't yet arrived.

When the front door opened, Dad carried two shot glasses in one palm and held an amber glass bottle by its neck with the other.

I took a shot glass from his extended hand. He sat and pulled the whiskey bottle cork. He filled our glasses and set the uncorked bottle on the porch floor in front of us. His toast was, "To absent friends, and to us, as no one else is likely to concern themselves with our welfare." We clicked our shots together, sharing the bonds of family and of men who'd volunteered to do what needed to be done.

We had just taken the first sip of our second shot when my mother came out onto the porch. She surveyed the scene. "Having a bit of the water of life, are you."

All of us knew a comment from a question.

"Eunice, can I pour you a tot?" Dad asked with a straight face.

"James, you know good and well, I never let liquor pass my lips."

Her answer brought smiles to our faces, as we tried not to expose our knowledge about the truth of her answer.

"I'm going to start making our dinner, so that one should be your last."

She got two deep nods in response.

I told her at the dinner table about the job prospect and my looming departure.

"We'll miss you, and you always have a place here." A mother to the last, but one who was used to sons leaving home.

The next day was taken up by planning and arranging my trip. My last day would be spent telling Bill and Dan about the perceived opportunity and my plan.

Also, I needed some new clothes. My two uniforms were put away and the things I'd left behind years ago no longer fit me or my needs. Left side pockets on pants no longer worked for me, and neither did a right inside jacket pocket. Loew's Dry Goods carried the best selection of men's clothing in town.

I came away with a tweed suit for my interview. Everything else I kept basic, since I didn't have a job yet. Two wool coats, two vests, two pairs of canvas trousers, suspenders and four sets of drawers and socks. I chose a long oiled canvas coat with its attached five-layer shoulder cape. The clerk called it a 'Garrick', but I knew it as a 'Coachman's coat.' I already had my black army boots, so I added another pair of heavy bull-hide work boots.

There were enough accessible pockets for cigars and matches. The vest pocket fit my watch, and two pants' pockets held my wallet and the muskrat-style pocketknife that was a graduation gift from Dad. My mother made quick work of altering the new long johns for me. I packed my Gladstone bag and was ready to go.

20. Barlow and Sanderson

April 1866

Bradley Barlow & Jared L. Sanderson

Photo by Matthew Brady

The Courtland Hotel was on a par with the hotels I'd seen in St. Louis. I'm sure there had been equally fine places in Atlanta before the Union army arrived.

The company had set up in two rented hotel rooms. Inside the first room, there were chairs set along two of the walls. A secretary sat behind a desk.

"Good morning," she smiled.

"I'm Duane Finch and I have an appointment."

'Yes Mr. Finch. Please take a seat. There is coffee if you want it while you wait." On the table sat a large silver urn. The two handles reminded me of a trophy or loving cup. The metal top rose into a spire.

"There is a restroom if you need to stop there before your interview." She pointed to a door off to her right.

I took one of three vacant chairs along the wall. At the moment, I seemed to be the only applicant. My back was to a window that looked out on the street below. Seeing no ashtrays, I took it as a hint that smoking by multiple men in this confined space was discouraged.

I didn't look at my watch, as that might make me seem impatient. After a good twenty minutes, the connecting door opened and out came a fella, hat in hand. "Good luck," he said to me as he passed out through the entry door.

The secretary left her desk and entered the other room. Then she was back in the doorway. "Mr. Finch, you can go in now."

The room had been altered from its usual use. The customary bed was gone and replaced by four chairs, two on each side of a finely crafted wooden table. My prospective employers rose from their seats behind the table.

"Please take a chair and be comfortable," said the taller of the two.

Bradley Barlow and Jared Sanderson took turns telling me how they'd started the business in 1863. They carried the mail on several short haul stage routes through Kansas and Missouri. They had the mail contract from St. Louis to Sacramento, California. The present hiring binge was part of a plan to compete for a second government mail contract, this one to California by the Santa Fe trail down through the New Mexico territory.

I could tell they were appraising me, the one-armed applicant, as they spoke. Finally, the topic of my arm came to the fore.

"What about your arm?" asked Barlow.

I told them about getting shot outside of Atlanta and what multiple doctors had told me about the injury being permanent.

"Mr. Finch, may I call you Duane?" This time, Jared Sanderson spoke for them.

"Sure."

"Brad and I both appreciate that you served, obviously with distinction, to come out as a Union Army officer. That said, your arm limits the jobs that we have available. Driver, stage guard and stockman are jobs you cannot do." I sat, waiting to be told, *thanks for coming in today, and best of luck in the future.*

Now Barlow took over. "Duane, I have some questions I'd like to ask, if I may?"

"Sure," I replied, and a stream of questions followed. They asked about the stability of my family back in West Union and the extent of my formal education. I told how I could read a map and lead a platoon of men. How I had volunteered immediately after Fort Sumter and not waited to be drafted into service. I drank, but not to excess and didn't have a wife or children.

When all of their questions had been answered, nothing had been said or done that suggested at their decision about employing me. "Duane, we need a minute. Would you wait in the other room? We'll come get you when Jared and I have decided."

So, I got up and walked out.

My wait was not long.

"Duane, come on back and take a seat," said Jared Sanderson. "There are lots of ways to be crippled. Some of the fellas we've interviewed were crippled, but we don't think you are crippled.

I wasn't understanding, and I guess he could tell.

"You, sir, lost the use of an arm. Some fellas have lost themselves to drink. Some are running from something: debts, a woman, the law, or a busted life. You seem to be a good man, a stable man, who is running to something. You speak well and have a friendly way about yourself." Pausing for a moment, Jared passed off to his partner.

"Duane, we think you would make a fine station agent, and we have a job for you at Paola, Kansas, if you want to join us?" It was a rhetorical question.

My answer came out quick. "Thank you, I'll take the job."

We shook hands before discussing detail about my pay and what was involved in being a station agent. I liked what I heard and nothing that I didn't. The job was waiting and the secretary, who now introduced herself as Edith, arranged my passage on a company stage. I'd stay the night at the Courtland at company expense and leave tomorrow. Tonight, I had something to write home about.

21. New Job, New Boss, New Town

Paola, Kansas, 1866

All I really knew about the state was 'Bloody Kansas', especially Quantrill's raid on Lawrence, where his raiders shot to death 200 men and boys. These civilians had held pro-Union sentiments, and that was enough for Quantrill. The land itself was flat, and during the forty-four-mile ride from Kansas City I didn't see enough water to baptize a bastard.

My first impressions of the town included that it had been Indian country until recently, Osage mostly. The two thousand inhabitants looked prosperous. It was half the size of Kansas City. It had the state's first college, the Kansas State Normal School, for training teachers.

There was no shortage of commerce: two department stores, an opera house, two breweries, hotels, livery, blacksmith, a Masonic lodge hall and churches. Baptists, Methodists and a large Catholic community. It was only August when we got our own newspaper, the Miami County Republican.

Main Street, Paola, Kansas

I'd had no trouble finding my way to our company office on Main Street since I exited the six-passenger Concord stagecoach right in front of it. While our two drivers pulled luggage from the boot, two other passengers and I were directed inside the stage depot office for a one-hour meal break.

Woodrow Clint, the station manager, welcomed the three of us and pointed the way to the dining room and restrooms. Everything was very much up to date: indoor plumbing, kitchen and dining room.

Clint was expecting me. "Duane Finch, welcome. Set your bag down over there in the corner. Get a meal and then come on back to my office." Pointing to a door over his left shoulder, he added, "Over yonder. Go see Mrs. Belcher."

The door led to the dining room. The food: fried chicken, pole beans cooked up with bacon, and biscuits with honey. Nothing I had to cut. Coffee, or cool water to drink. Lunch was served by the black cook, who introduced herself as Miss Bessie. With her three guests served, she addressed us. "I hope you enjoy my cooking. If you need another piece of that chicken or another biscuit, you tell me." And with that, she marched back into her kitchen.

The food was good. Her ample girth had hinted at the promise of her cooking, and it did not disappoint. My two traveling companions from Kansas City, George Satterfield and his wife Hilda, excused themselves and exited the dining room, heading toward their appointment with the stage.

When I'd finished, I stuck my head in the kitchen doorway. "Miss Bessie, you are indeed a good cook." That brought a smile to her round black face as she wiped her hands on an embroidered towel then straightened her apron. "Thank you, sir."

"Miss Bessie, I'm Duane Finch and I'll be working here for Mr. Clint." Her smile broadened, and she held up her index finger in a 'wait a moment' gesture, and, with a turn of her head, called out. "Hercules, come out here and meet Mr. Finch."

* * *

At the back of the kitchen, a door opened. Beyond it appeared hints of a residence. Standing in the doorway was a short black man. If this was Hercules, he'd been named either as a joke or more likely in hopes of a new son being large, strong and fearless. His posture was erect and his face alert but not displaying any particular

117

emotion. First, he scanned the kitchen. Taking a long look at the strange man opposite his wife, Hercules walked over to her side.

We spent our first face-to-face moments in silent contemplation of the other. At five foot-six, I was not used to being taller than anyone, but my smile and offer of my right hand broke the tension. "Duane Finch, pleased to meet you."

There was no hesitation in his response. "Sir," and his hand met mine. There was no obsequiousness in the man standing before me. Quite the opposite, his bearing conveyed dignity and self-assurance. *This man has been in the military. He is a giver of orders. Except perhaps to his big wife.*

"Mr. Finch, sir, it is a pleasure to meet you, and welcome to Paola."

I smiled and nodded as we both stepped closer and shook hands.

"I manage the stations animals. sir."

What the hell? This man would need to stand on a box to put a bridle on a horse or mule. But I'd keep my opinions to myself.

I addressed my employee by his last name, as a sign of respect. "Mr. Belcher, what did you do before the war?"

"I was a jockey, sir. That's how I learned to manage horses. I looks 'um right in the eye and I talks to 'um. They likes that sir, because, well, you know, in the eyes of the Lord, we are both beasts."

Being a man of faith myself, I liked his response. Then it was my turn to answer his questions.

"Your arm, sir? The war, sir? Do it pain you some, sir?" As quick as the third question escaped his lips, Miss Bessie joined in. Asking a white boss anything, let alone something about an obvious disability, was risky and potentially disastrous.

Trying to read the situation, I spoke up to calm the kitchen.

"No, no, that's fine Miss Bessie." I shifted my focus back to her pocket-sized Hercules. "Shot through the shoulder at the Battle of Atlanta. I don't have any pain."

He nodded in recognition and Miss Bessie exhaled in relief. Her husband had not shown concern. He'd asked respectfully, had held eye contact and was clearly not afraid of a white boss. I'm sure he'd seen many.

I like this man.

"Your wife is an excellent cook. I need to get back to work and see Mr. Clint. I have a lot to learn about the stage business. So be patient with me while I learn the job."

"Yes sir, I will. And thank you for fighting to make us colored folks free." Then, quite to my surprise, his right hand went up and he offered a proper salute. I didn't know quite what to do, so I returned the salute and left the kitchen.

22. Learning the Job

1866

I found the door to Woodrow Clint's office open, and knocked on the door frame before entering. He motioned for me to come in. "Have a seat," and he started with a question. "Did the bosses share their expansion plans with you?"

I replied, "Yes."

"So, you know the long-term plan. Now, all we have to do is get there.

"The company has twenty short-haul routes now. In Kansas, we run from Kansas City to Fort Scott and St. Louis. That was where they started. The operation has begun to move south; Fort Larned, Kansas, to Fort Lyon, Colorado, with routes connecting to Denver, Pueblo, Fort Bent and Trinidad. Then, we can compete for the mail run through New Mexico, Las Vegas and into California.

"Each expansion of routes means new stage stops to locate, staff and provide with stock. There are lots of moving parts to expanding. Their ultimate goal requires us to get a route over Raton Pass, the southernmost way across the great divide, and connect to Santa Fe in the New Mexico Territory."

Clint paused and stood up. I continued to sit, as he poured himself a glass of water from a covered ceramic carafe, sitting on a back bar in the corner. The heat from outside was only partially minimized by the high ceilings of all the rooms I'd seen thus far. "Water, Duane?"

I gratefully accepted the offer, and he poured a second glass, returned to his desk and passed one to me. My sip was a pleasant surprise. It was cooler than evaporation would produce. Somewhere nearby was an icehouse, either ours or owned by another business

"Anyway, Bradley and Jared's grand plan is to connect from Santa Fe to California. They want the government mail contract for the southern route. With their system now connecting from St. Louis to California, through Colorado, the goldfields are attractors for passengers, freight and mail."

Big plans indeed.

"The bosses are cautious businessmen. So, their plan will come about in stages: gradual expansion, one small route at a time. They want you to learn the business from me here at Paola. When you and the company are both ready, you'll take over one of the new stations as manager.

"That's a lot to chew on and you've just arrived. Let's get you settled in today; give you a chance to catch your breath; look over the town a bit." Clint rose from his seat, signaling our meeting was over. He walked around the desk past me. "Follow me now, and I'll show you to your quarters. "

Down the hall we went, stopping first at the restrooms. Inside the designated Men's Room, Clint led me to a locked door, behind which was a claw-footed bathtub. "That's for you, but not the passengers, except with special permission from me, or now from you." Back out into the hall, we moved to the second of two doors down.

Woodrow extracted a key from his shirt pocket, opened the door and passed the key to me. Bed, bureau, and desk partially furnished the room. Two chairs, one straight-backed for writing at the desk and the other, a padded wingback. One nightstand, a wash table with a basin and pitcher, and three lamps completed the picture. The room smelled clean and one curtained window showed a view of blooming hollyhocks outside.

The tour concluded, Woodrow Clint told me to come to his office at eight the next morning. Then he left, and the balance of the day was mine. I unpacked my Gladstone bag and sat down on the bed, testing the mattress. As I did, my heel nudged a covered chamber pot, placed discretely under the bed. My 'thunder mug' for overnight use.

On my way out, I asked through his office door. "Hercules Belcher, did he serve during the war?"

Clint squared himself in the doorway. "Hercules was the Sergeant Major for the 1st Kansas Colored Infantry."

* * *

Outside on Main Street, I began to explore, reversing the direction that I'd seen as our stage rolled in. The street-level door to the

Masonic lodge was locked, but the bulletin showed me the day and time of the regular meeting: first Tuesday of every month at 7 PM. Moving on down along the sidewalk, I found a nearby dry goods store and an apothecary, complete with a soda fountain.

I'd shed my coat and tie back in my new room but had kept my hat, a straw boater style, as protection from the afternoon sun. Much as I might enjoy a beer, I chose not to make my first introduction to the community from inside a tavern. A soda water would have to suffice.

Inside were high ceilings, and open transom windows accessed by a perimeter catwalk above shelf-lined walls cooled the apothecary. I took a seat at the marble-topped counter and asked the white-clad counter man for a large sarsaparilla. I watched him draw the dark brown liquid from a built-in squirt container and charge the heavy glass mug with sparking water to a frothy fill. With my first pull, the familiar flavor and cool interior of the store set my mind to rest. Paola, Kansas, and my new job were both going to suit me.

There were groups of unescorted women in twos and threes, enjoying a fountain drink. Other women were drinking from china cups: tea probably. Two middle-aged men having an animated conversation occupied one of the round marble tables at the back. Everyone was well dressed, not fancy mind you, but no overalls or chaps. Business people or church ladies, from the look of them.

* * *

Next on my list of things to do or places to locate was a cigar store. With my mug now empty, I paid my nickel and headed down the street, on the hunt for one of life's simple pleasures: a smoke.

One corner further down the street, a wooden Indian stood watch outside a shop. Over his head hung a painted wooden sign showing a calabash-style pipe with a graceful spire of smoke rising from its bowl. Gold capital letters on the window glass spelled out "Tobacco Emporium." Beneath the large gold letters of the name was a smaller script admonition. "If we don't have it, you wouldn't want it."

A prayer had indeed been answered. My nose immediately registered the sweet smells of tobaccos. Golden Virginia, rich dark burley and the aromatics of Latakia and Perique, all hit their own distinctive notes in a symphony for my nose.

Inside the shop, three sides of the room had glass-topped display cases. Well-stocked shelves stood behind each case. In the first cases on the long right-hand side were open boxes of cigars. Every size and shape of cigar I'd ever seen lay before me, along with exotic ones I'd never seen.

Across the room sat an equally daunting choice of pipe styles from Pot to Billiard, half–bent to full bend, to the giant Calabash. Even at a distance, the rich red of cherry wood, dark briar and white imported meerschaum were all obvious to meet any combination of preferred size, shape and material.

Accessories were displayed behind the pipes. There were humidors and pipe racks. Both glass and ceramic ashtrays were on display. Shelves of glass tobacco canisters filled an entire vertical row of shelving.

My eyes were about to roll back. All I wanted was a smoke, and the myriad of choices was too much to contemplate. Fortunately, I was saved by the appearance of the proprietor from out of the back.

"Gabriel Bench, welcome."

I gave a relieved response. "Duane Finch."

Bench nodded in recognition. "How can I help you, Mr. Finch?"

All the visible choices had quickly convinced me of how little I actually knew about cigars. To avoid displaying my ignorance, I retrieved one of what I'd been smoking and held it up for his review.

Mr. Bench studied the cigar for a few moments and then asked, "May I?" and reached out.

I surrendered the cigar.

He rolled it between his fingers and passed it slowly under his nose before returning it to me.

"Yes," was all he said. He turned and soon came back with a wooden box, which he set down on the display case and opened. Immediately the smell was familiar, as well as the shape.

Noting my approval, he made an unexpected offer. "Try one, on me. If you like the smoke, good. A nickel each, dollar a box."

The proprietor gestured for me to take a seat in one of the leather chairs in the center of the room. Six chairs formed an oval around a low, round table. The dark wood of the table and chairs all matched.

Six round amber glass ashtrays ringed the outer edge of the table. A match caddy and striker plate were centered within reach of all the smokers.

I took a seat at the nominal head of the table. The war, still fresh in my past, made it uncomfortable for me to sit with my back to a route for someone to sneak up on me. I bit the rolled end off the cigar. Then I struck a match and put flame to the cylinder of tobacco. The cigar drew nicely, signaling a firm, even pack to the tobacco. The first draws of smoke were aromatic and sweet. Happily, the smoke neither burned nor bit my mouth.

Mr. Bench watched from behind his counter, trying to judge my reaction. "How is that for you, Mr. Finch?" I savored another draw of the smoke before removing the cigar and answering. "Very nice. It smokes cool and draws easy."

"Good. I thought you might like those." Then the conversation changed. "May I ask about your arm?" He didn't wait for my answer, which was not a problem. "Did that happen fighting Indians, Mexicans or rebels?"

"Shot in the shoulder at Atlanta."

Bench winced, his lips drawing tight.

"Well, I appreciate every one of you who put on the blue. I lost friends at Lawrence to Quantrill and his vicious border trash."

I made no response but to tap some white ash off my smoke.

"May I ask, what brings you to town?"

"A job. I'm going to be the assistant stage manager for Woodrow Clint. And I'll take a box of these beauties."

Bench nodded back. "Take your time. Finish your smoke if you like. I'll have your box at the counter whenever you are ready."

I finished my smoke, leaving the cigar butt and burned match in the nearest ashtray. I made a point of thanking Bench for his hospitality. Handing over a dollar coin, I shook my host's hand and left the store.

23. Learning Nuts from Bolts

1866-67 Paola, Kansas

For the Union, the years after the Civil War were a great time of optimism, expansion and opportunity. Americans were moving west, where land was free, and every mountain or stream was a potential gold or silver claim. Some came on horseback or in a Conestoga wagon, but many came by stage.

The more rapid movement of people, mail or money was either by rail, where available, or by stagecoach. Barlow and Sanderson saw an opportunity. By moving to where the rails were not and by running the short-line connections to and from rails and rivers, we made ourselves essential.

Barlow and Sanderson Stagecoach

So many moving parts and I needed to learn all of them. And this was only the beginning, as it turned out. The other component of this three-legged stool was timing, along with space and money. Each station agent was in many ways a franchisee, affiliated with the parent company, but mostly making his own decisions on a local basis.

Woodrow introduced me to our bookkeeper, Horace, and our two clerks. Miss Eve Brooks and Mrs. Charlotte Scott were the ones who checked on the implementation of Woodrow's orders and directives. They booked the passengers and kept the operation running, despite what they allowed the men in charge to believe.

Paola was a station 'Depot,' the hub for a larger area that also needed multiple 'station houses.' Depots had a regional manager. They were the centers that received and discharged mail and freight from the several government contracts held by Barlow and Sanderson.

After Woodrow had laid out the organization, he told me about their coaches. To traverse the rough, frontier roads and trails over vast plains, over mountain passes and through storms and desert dust, they needed a vehicle up to the task. The answer: the Concord Coach, so named after its place of manufacture in New Hampshire. They were not cheap, at over $1,100 average per coach, Free on Board (FOB) Concord, New Hampshire. Then, at the buyer's expense, the coach came by sea to the nearest port, finally to be received dockside.

Each coach, all 2,000 pounds of it, eight feet high and almost six feet wide, was handmade of the finest, sturdiest woods. Every piece of leather for the rear luggage cover and side panels of the driver's box was premium steer hide. No space got wasted. Side racks on the roof secured cargo or extra passengers liking to save money.

Inside, padded upholstered seats softened the bumpy ride with comfortable seating for nine passengers. High racks held wool blankets and buffalo robes as defenses against the winter cold. They had sliding glass windows in the coach doors and damask-lined leather curtains rolled up on all the side windows.

The exterior side panels were painted in vivid red, yellow, and black. Gilt scrollwork bracketed panels emblazoned with the coach company name, or route names, such as "Santa Fe Express." If the company had the contract, 'U. S. Mail' would be painted on the doors. The driver's name was painted on the side panels of the driver's box.

The cost of a delivered coach was reflected in the fares we charged. Distance and conditions of the route also figured in. Were we likely to meet Indians we either had to outfight or outrun. Sandy, snowy rivers to cross or narrow mountain roads were all considered in setting our fares, Woodrow explained. Our posted price for St. Louis to Denver was $175, while St Louis to California was $325 for the nineteen-day trip.

The west, by any measure, is a wild and dangerous place. Travelers boarded the stage at their own risk. Indian attacks and road agents were real and constant threats. The passengers were encouraged, for the good of all, to travel armed.

* * *

Paola was our regional stock yard, where replacement horses and mules waited until needed. I learned from Hercules that our stock pens held hundreds of animals at all times. Hercules took a proprietary pride in his corner of the operation.

Inside his hay barn were seven tons of hay, a one-day supply to feed the five hundred-fifty horses and mules in our network of relay stations and station houses. Between what we bought and grew at our station houses, three thousand tons of hay were needed annually.

The horses for the teams of four or six were not chosen for beauty, but for size and strength. These came to Hercules as green stock from a host of reputable brokers. Under his care, they learned the art of pulling as part of a team.

He supervised the blacksmiths, farriers, harness makers, cartwrights and carpenters that kept the coaches running. So too, he kept a stock of harness, coach blankets and buffalo robes on hand to be disbursed as and where needed.

A traveling blacksmith, complete with forge, visited the relay stations regularly. A dozen teamsters with freight wagons kept the stops supplied with everything from coffee and beans to livestock and tack. Messages about their needs for replacement tack or horses came to us through our driver's network. Beans, bullets and hay arrived regularly to keep men and animals safe and well fed.

* * *

127

Each leg of a trip was twelve to fifteen miles, and the team ran non-stop to the next relay station. There, a fresh team, already in harness, got hooked to the coach for the next leg of travel. Relay stations were mostly remote: just three men, a sod or log cabin and a horse corral.

The coach traveled for up to twelve hours per day, covering sixty to seventy miles in total. The final stop came at a station house. A hot dinner, usually prepared by the stage agent's wife, could be purchased. Two or three small cabins at each stop provided sleeping accommodations for passengers and crew. Each station house also had its own blacksmith, hay field, barn, and carriage repair shop. These were good folk running our station houses, and we ate well at their tables.

While the passengers and crew ate and slept, the agent and his helpers changed one coach for another. Baggage was reloaded into the new coach, and the axles and wheel hubs of the other coach received greasing and any other needed repairs. Just another 'moving part' among the many that I learned about.

* * *

Hercules was indeed a master horseman. I witnessed him in action when he and Woodrow took me around to each stop in our chain of relays and station houses. Hercules approached a large coach horse, and the great beast shied as the stranger neared.

He stopped his advance and withdrew a carrot from a back pocket and held it out toward the wary animal. Then he waited. Soon the horse caught the smell of food. Hercules knew that the tempting morsel, held so near, would interrupt the animal's initial flight response. Still, the former jockey didn't approach. He let the smell of food do its work.

When the horse's eyes were fixed on the treat, the little man lay the carrot flat in the palm of his hand and took one step closer. Again he paused, observing the animal's response, but ever slowly, he brought the orange treat closer, talking softly to the big animal as he approached.

Finally, his patience was rewarded as the horse's brown lips reached the food and Hercules' other hand stroked its muzzle.

Our system presently connected with the St. Louis routes at St. Joe, Missouri, and extended south as far as Pueblo, Colorado. At both station houses, short lines led to smaller outlying towns, such as Pueblo to Denver and Trinidad to Fort Bent.

Both Woodrow and Hercules carried leather notebooks containing the names of every employee at each relay station and station house. Woodrow gave me a blank notebook of my own. "Keep each relay or house on its own page, so you can make changes as needed." His suggestion, I soon discovered, was pure gold. I would never have been able to remember all the people and places.

Here's the deal: think in terms of the distances.

Paola, Kansas to Pueblo, Colorado is 550 miles. Pueblo to Denver is another 113 miles. Add on Trinidad, Colorado, for another 86 miles and Trinidad to Fort Bent at La Junta, 80 miles further. Now, divide those distances by 12 to 15 miles for a relay station, and add a station house every 70 miles. I had long ago run out of ass before we ran out of miles to ride.

* * *

The relay stations seemed a world apart, often isolated in rugged locations. The three-man crews were a rough, scraggly-bearded bunch who mostly introduced themselves by nicknames. Between Shorty, Big Nick and just plain Joe, no last names were offered. My two teachers told me not to ask. How many of the lot traded a prison for the isolation of a relay station was left unexamined.

"Tell 'um about your Saturday bath, Big Nick," said Woodrow.

"We take blankets and drawers out and put on the anthill in back, so the ants can eat the lice and bedbugs. Then the next morning we bring em all back in. Least wise we can see ants and knock 'em off."

Big Nick offered sleeping space on the floor inside the sod relay station shack for me and Woodrow. "Your darkie sleeps outside," he said. Woodrow and I exchanged looks. No words required, as we both knew there was nothing to discuss. Woodrow noticed the change in my posture and the set of my jaw. He turned and held his hands out, palms down. We were outnumbered and for Big Nick and his crew, once an asshole, always an asshole.

"We'll sleep out here with Hercules. Thanks all the same."

This part of the territory had been fought over during the war back in 1862. Old memories, grudges and long-held beliefs died hard, and died slow.

I'd made water for the final time and lay down on my blanket, with a saddle for a pillow. Hercules lay on my right, and Woodrow was already asleep on my left. "I kind of figured that they kept some of the lice for pets, gave em names and raced them," I said, keeping my voice low. "What do you think?"

"I was kind of thinking that Little Joe was their pet, except they call him Josephine when we're not here."

"Well, he is a cute little bugger. Something else though; I think I need to add a pistol to my wardrobe."

24. The Race is On

1868

In November 1867, the Union Pacific railroad reached into Colorado at Julesburg, and I changed my mind about who was to be our competition. When I started, I thought that Butterfield and other stage lines were our foes. Now I knew our true race for markets was with a host of rail lines.

Starting in that same month, we extended our line from Trinidad over the Raton Pass. This took us into the New Mexico territory via the old Santa Fe Trail and on west into California. In May, the government offered the mail contract for the southern route, but our long-time competition got the contract.

My bosses had moved their headquarters south to Denver and were continuing to expand and adjust routes. Among the adjustments was changing a route through Bent's Fort and thus cutting a hundred miles and one full day off the trip from Denver to Trinidad.

With eighteen months of my guided tutorial about our company under my belt, I understood how we operated, where we were, and where we were going. The mail contracts were hugely profitable, as were our short-haul branch lines. In the short route arena, we were easily able to compete with rail lines. Short lines required fewer relay stations and station houses.

We extended our lines the 84 miles from Trinidad to Fort Garland and from Pueblo to Fort Lyons. BG Christopher 'Kit' Carson had been in command at Fort Garland since 1866 and tasked with pacifying the Utes. The general had recently returned from shepherding a group of Ute chiefs to Washington for a treaty signing.

In mid-May, just one month after the death of his third wife, the general passed away at Fort Lyons. I felt a kinship to Carson, who was also a Master Mason. I traveled to his funeral at Boggsville, three miles outside of Las Animas. I stood graveside as the general was laid to rest wearing the unstained purity of his white lamb-skin apron over his dress uniform. I only wish I'd had the honor to sit in lodge at least once with the man.

* * *

I followed newspaper accounts about the formation and developments of the Grand Army of the Republic (GAR) Veterans' Benevolent Organization. It was modeled after the first veterans' organization, the Society of the Cincinnati, founded by George Washington in 1783. I supported any group that could speak with one voice for the more than 400,000 Union civil war veterans.

In November 1866, their first convention, chaired by General Stephen Hurlbut, drafted a constitution for the organization. In May 1868, at the National Encampment in Philadelphia, the Commander-in-Chief of the GAR, General John Logan, declared May 30th, "Decoration Day." He urged all veterans to honor their dedication to the Union annually on this date.

I saw an opportunity. This could be a good time, what with the national coverage and all, to start a GAR Post here in Paola. There were war widows and orphaned children, left with nothing after their soldiers had lost their lives in Union service. Myself, I was doing all right, but the hundreds of thousands of veterans who'd given years of their lives should by rights get some type of pension for their service.

But the war was over, and the politicians didn't want to pay. They had moved on, even if the Union veterans had not. The veterans here in Paola needed to speak with one voice, to keep from being forgotten. I wrote to General Logan at the GAR Washington D.C. headquarters and asked to open a Post in Paola.

In one week, I had my answer in a letter signed by the Executive Secretary for the GAR.

Dear Lt. Finch,

Thank you for contacting us. The GAR appreciates your interest and your service. Send me a list of twelve Union veterans, identified by full name and their former military unit. We will authenticate the list and then issue a charter, officially recognizing your Post by name and number.

Very truly yours,

Everett Daws

I put an ad in the Miami County Republic.

Union Veterans

Join the GAR to have our voices heard! Contact DD Finch at the Barlow and Sanderson Depot Office.

In no time at all, we had a dozen Union veterans signed up for the GAR. Among the veterans expressing interest was Col. Maxwell McCaslin, 15th West Virginia Infantry. He had been a Pennsylvania State Senator before the war. I sent back our list of names to Secretary Daws and, by popular votes, recommended our Post be named after the colonel. Three weeks later, we received our charter; McCaslin Post #117. We elected McCaslin our first Post Commander.

25. A Princess in Paola

1870

The Kansas State Normal School, our teacher's college, sat just three blocks off Paola's Main street. A four-story brick building rose in the middle of a two-square-block campus. Surrounding it were lawns and shade trees, all inside a low, wrought-iron fence. Behind the administrative and instructional building was a three-story student dormitory and a smaller, two-story residence for unmarried female faculty.

I was sharing a smoke with Gabriel Bench in his emporium when she walked in. Long blue skirt, white blouse with puffy upper sleeves and a pillbox hat. Bench excused himself, rose and spoke as he walked over to his sales counters. "Yes, ma'am, how can I help you today?"

"I'm looking for pipes." The voice was bigger than the petite five-foot tall speaker.

"A gift for your husband or father, I'm guessing."

The question brought forth a small snicker from the customer before she responded. "No, it's for me." And her posture grew even more erect, if that was possible. "That is, if you do sell to ladies, sir, or should I take my business elsewhere?"

It was a challenge more than a question. *I'm petite and female. And I'll smoke if I want!*

I watched Gabriel as he gave her his full attention. If he was surprised or taken aback, neither showed. "Yes, ma'am, we certainly sell to the entire smoking community, including ladies. I have an extensive selection of pipes for you to view. If you would follow me, please," and he motioned across the shop to the cases and displays of pipes. He led, and she followed to the large collection of options.

Turning to face her, he asked, "Do you have any style in mind?"

She answered immediately with the confidence of a practiced smoker. "Small bowl, quarter-bent, long stem and briar."

Gabriel nodded. He paused, apparently considering what among his selection met her several specifics.

Then he nodded again and pursed his lips. He knew just where to look among his many cases, displays and back stock of pipes. He raised an index finger in an 'ah ha' gesture and removed a wooden drawer of pipes from the hidden storage space below the glass-topped case.

He set the drawer in front of her and stepped back to await a response.

She studied the tray of pipes laid before her, then picked up a choice.

What Gabriel Bench and I saw next were clearly not the actions of a novice pipe smoker. First, she held the pipe in her hand, judging its weight. Heavy pipes are hard on the jaw and require a constant hand on them. Her fingers stroked the surfaces of the briar bowl, checking for tell-tale hints of imperfections in the grain of the wood.

Next, she raised the bowl almost to her lips and blew air into it, holding the palm of her other hand facing the open end of the pipe stem. She was checking the air flow through the bowl and stem to see if the pipe, when lit, would draw easily.

Gabriel gave a silent nod at her practiced means of testing the pipe. Only a first-time smoker would put a pipe stem into their mouth and return it, uncleaned, to a display.

Then she repeated the same series of tests on three more pipes before making her selection.

"This one please," she announced, holding up a Peterson brand pipe of Irish manufacture.

Bench and I traded glances, signaling how impressed we were with her diligence. Then, in true merchant fashion, he continued selling.

"Tobacco, ma'am?"

She answered in the affirmative. "Yes, I'll need two ounces of a light Virginia blend for the break-in."

And again, Bench signaled his approval. "Ah, the perfect choice for a smooth break-in of bowl, to help it season and build up an ash crust." He turned and removed a canister from the shelves behind the pipe display. He took it down to a small balance scale on the far-left corner of the counter. A two-ounce weight went on one scale pan. He took golden strands of tobacco from the canister to the scale. When the desired ounces were measured out, he carefully poured them into an oilskin tobacco pouch that folded twice over for an airtight seal.

Ever a merchant, next he inquired, "tamping tool, matches or pipe cleaners?" All of which the petite customer declined.

He directed the lady with her pipe and tobacco in hand to his cash register, they settled up, and he placed her purchases in a paper bag. "Thank you so much. I am your host, Gabriel Bench, and it's a pleasure to have your business. Please come again when you are in need of anything more for your smoking pleasure." The lady smiled and offered her hand.

"I'm Mrs. Sarah Fain," and then she departed with a polite, "Thank you."

As Gabriel and I watched her go, the ever-growing ash tip of my cigar finally reached my fingers. I let out a "yip" in pain and surprise, knocking off the hot ash as the cigar stub tumbled into one of the tabletop ashtrays. *Fascinating woman.* My thought was interrupted when Bench snickered a bit. He leaned in towards me, "she wears a wedding ring."

Shit.

26. Sarah Fain

October - December, 1868

The next time I saw Mrs. Fain, she was leaving the Plum Creek Methodist Church, over on the south side of town. I'd been seated in one of the back pews while she must have been somewhere in front.

Today she wore more modest, somber colors. Layers of gray, beginning with the charcoal skirt and topped by the silver-gray pattern of a paisley-print shawl. She paused on the church steps and removed the sheer black veil that had covered her head. For the first time, I noticed her hair, a deep chestnut amber.

We were just one week away from Halloween. The leaves were turning and had begun to fall as the days, while still dry, had turned cool but not yet cold. She was unaccompanied and had adopted a leisurely pace back towards town. Luckily, I was headed in the same direction. I took the same route home, choosing to respect the distance between us. Attentions from a stranger could easily be mistaken for the ploy of a common masher or worse.

Where Wallace Park crossed East Osage Street, Mrs. Fain left the sidewalk and moved onto one of the park's gravel paths. She stopped and took a seat on a wrought-iron bench visible from the street that faced into the park. The hour now being just after eleven, the morning was pleasantly warm as other church attendees passed on their walks home, while others in couples ventured off, hand in hand, into the park.

I was two blocks back and soon would have to make the choice. Walk on or turn in and approach? I slowed my pace, the better to judge the lady's mood. Would she be looking up, looking for the singing birds in the canopy of trees? Or would her head be bent, her eyes cast down, perhaps thinking of a lost love? I wanted to meet this mystery woman and considered my first approach which, if not done thoughtfully, would probably be my only chance.

Finally, at the park, I had to choose. I'd not approached a woman, any woman, since the one back in Pittsburg. *Sorry, I don't do gimps.* The line had never left me.

I took the path, knowing that I'd feel worse about failing to try than failing in my approach. The curved path allowed me to come in from the left rather than uncomfortably from behind her field of view. I watched her remove pipe and tobacco pouch from a clutch purse and set about filling the bowl with tobacco. *Yes!* I took a cigar from my coat pocket as I walked on, timing my arrival to match her need for fire.

She'd packed her bowl and rolled the tobacco pouch closed as I took my first puff of smoke, the lit stick match still in hand. "May I offer you a light?"

As her gaze shifted from the pipe to me, she hesitated before speaking. "You'd better do it now, before you burn your fingers," and she leaned toward me.

I held the match above the pipe bowl as she moved the bowl side to side, drawing the flame down with each inhalation. *OUCH!* Just in time, when I couldn't hold the match any longer, it was safe to blow it out.

"Thank you." She took successive draws on the pipe to fully light its tobacco.

I remained standing, smiling back.

The woman who looked up at me had a fine-boned delicacy to her face. Freckles dotted her high cheeks and across the bridge of her small nose. Her eyes were green, and she'd walked with confidence. Slim but not gaunt, everything about her captivated me under that crown of chestnut hair. *Don't push it.*

"Well, enjoy your smoke, ma'am," and I pivoted on my heels, ready to walk on.

"Did you enjoy the sermon?" she asked. The question surprised me, not by its content, but by her having asked. I took the panatela from my mouth.

"Today's sermon reminded me that Christ died for all of humanity, not just a limited group, and so everyone is entitled to God's love and grace. I struggle with that sometimes." I paused, staring down at my cigar.

"Because of the war?" she asked. I gave no response until she lowered the pipe stem from her lips and cradled the bowl in her delicate hands. "Because of your arm?"

A nod was my first response. "All of it," I said.

"I struggle with that lesson too," she said back to me.

My cigar was done, and it was time to leave. "Thank you for the pleasure of your company. Oh, I apologize, I'm Duane Finch."

"No apology required, Mr. Finch, and thank you for the light."

* * *

The following Sunday, she left the Plum Creek Church alone again. I'd waited outside, hoping to see her. She had not yet spoken her name, and the supposed Mr. Fain, though suggested by the wedding ring, was still absent from the picture.

Instead of hoping to repeat last Sunday's chance meeting, I'd speak to her here, safely in sight of the church and the crowd of congregants. Today she was all in blue, including the veil that had covered her head while inside the church.

"Ah…I wondered if you might let me buy you a soda drink at Maul's drugstore sometime next week."

She smiled, perhaps because of the week before. Or because I'd been polite and perhaps not immune to her beauty?

"Why Mr. Finch, happy Sunday. I am just on my way home, with a brief stop in the park." And she offered up a knowing smile as to the purpose of her stop. So, I broached the question.

"Will your husband be joining you today?" Caught unawares by my question, she hesitated and, knitting her brow, offered up a questioning look. I pointed to the ring on the third finger of her left hand.

She inhaled, her chin and her lips pulling into a straight line, neither smile nor frown, as she raised her hand and stared momentarily at the ring. Straightening her head, she returned my gaze. "My husband died at Newtonia, Missouri, in September 1862. He was part of the 10th Kansas Volunteer Infantry."

The conversation had taken a dark turn, and I needed to change it. "So, would a soda at Maul's be something you'd like to share?" That did the trick, and she finally smiled in my direction.

"I am a faculty member at the Normal School. My day doesn't end until our last class is over, at 3:30. I think I have time in my day for a soda at Maul's. I reside in the single women's dormitory on

139

campus and need to be back by dinner, which they serve promptly at five in the evening."

"So yes, then?"

And she confirmed with her own "Yes."

It was my turn now. "When would you like?" And we agreed on Tuesday at 4.

* * *

When I arrived, she was already seated at one of the small, round marble-topped tables. She had been on my mind for almost two full weeks and had yet to tell me her first name. Which I already knew, of course, but having it offered to me was an important difference from overhearing it. We exchanged quick greetings, as a young, white-clad server came to the table to take our orders.

She ordered a cherry fizz, and I picked grape. The gasogene machine on the counter forced carbon dioxide bubbles from its top glass globe down into the water in the lower globe. Mr. Maul, the seemingly ageless pharmacist, pumped two squirts of our chosen flavor syrups into glasses, over small amounts of ice from his own icehouse. Then he filled each with the carbonated water, inserted straws and brought the cold, fizzy sodas to our small table.

As we drank, I worked at not staring, no matter how much I wanted just to look at her freckled cheeks and chestnut hair. I listened as she answered my questions, and I in return answered hers. All our topics were safe. Where had we grown up and where were our people? Did we like our jobs? And she told me her name was Sarah, with an 'H.'

She'd delivered the clarification about her name with a smile. Knowing that the lady had a sense of humor put me more at ease. I liked her a lot and boy did I want her to like me.

Finally silent, we sipped our sodas, untroubled by the pause, which ended with the slurping sounds of our straws emptying the last liquids. When our cheeks finished sucking in for the last sweet drops, we smiled across the table.

"I had best get back. I have a stage to meet in the next half-hour."

On my feet first, I stepped around the table and helped her up from the white wrought-iron chair. As I walked her towards the

140

school, she hummed something unfamiliar. We parted at my office door, two blocks from her residential school. But not before I asked.

"May I see you again? I'd like that very much."

"Why yes, I'd like that too," and she was smiling now. My heart raced with unfocused, but happy thoughts.

"When, then?"

"Thursday would be nice."

"Can we make it a lunch at Howard's Café?"

"I'm sorry, my time for lunch is limited, and so I'll have to content myself with sodas at Maul's for the time being." Her answer was fine with me, if not what I'd hoped for.

"So, we meet back at Maul's in two days' time?" I waited nervously for any positive answer.

Finally it came. "All right."

* * *

I judged our second meeting a success; she told me to call her Sarah.

"I'm Duane or DD. Mr. Finch was my father." And that made her laugh.

Her people were all in or around Milwaukee, and that we were both born there made us smile. I was two years her senior. She'd been a bride at eighteen and a childless widow by twenty, her only pregnancy cut short by a stress-induced miscarriage when her husband died in the war.

Then came the residential teachers' college, one of a very few options for a young widow. The school filled her needs for a residence, future job prospects and, most of all, respect from the man's world. I told her about my family back in West Union and how I'd come to Paola for the Barlow and Sanderson stage line.

Our comfort level seemed to grow. She wanted to hear about the war. What it was like? Was I afraid? Were the rebels all awful? Sometimes we waxed serious about why the war had been so cruel. Sometimes she seemed lifted from the shadows that at moments darkened her soul.

"Oh, and were the Tennessee and Mississippi girls pretty?" she asked me once. I answered quickly. "No, they are all about as pretty as a mud fence. Not at all like you." The answer must have been right, or at least it pleased Sarah, as shown by a smile that illuminated her face. If I was doing nothing right, at least I wasn't doing anything wrong.

After another week of afternoon get togethers at Maul's, Sarah asked if I'd still like to take her to lunch, on a Saturday. As the November days grew shorter, and the afternoons moved from cool to chilly, an early lunch appealed to her. Followed, of course, by a shared smoke over in Wallace Park.

I jumped at the chance. But my duties at work gave me a moment's pause. I had more responsibilities, as Woodrow Clint became comfortable with my progress up the learning curve. I ran the day-to-day operations of the depot while he happily concentrated on supply and contractual issues. I'd spoken too soon.

"I have a stage to meet at noon. Would you be able to survive till one o'clock?"

"That's asking an awful lot, Mr. Finch. I'd need time to think that over. I'll let you know." She'd delivered the lines in perfect deadpan, her tone a mix of business with just a hint of disappointment.

My heart sank. What was I to do? Worse yet, it was time for her to go, as dinnertime approached. I got up and was pulling out her chair when she let me off her tenterhooks. "I'll meet you there, Saturday at one."

"You are awful," I exclaimed, and she turned her head just enough for me to see the smile at the corner of her mouth. Her final words as she walked away came over her shoulder, "Yes, I am, and you better get used to it."

* * *

Saturday's lunch was at Howard's, the nicest dining room in Paola. We were seated at a table with a linen tablecloth and napkins. Outside, the weather had moved from cool to chilly during the day and cold at night.

We both chose the Howard's special: hearty, thick barley-and-vegetable soup served with a loaf of house-baked bread, still hot from the oven. It was wonderful, both the food and the conversation. Sarah Fain was becoming more comfortable with me, and I

142

continued to grow in admiration for her beauty and inner strength. After lunch, I helped her into her heavy cloth coat and I donned my shearling jacket.

We walked down Main to Osage and into Wallace Park. We chose to keep walking while enjoying our after-lunch smokes. Stopping, we faced each other as shelter from the breeze while she lit her pipe. When she got a good light going, I knew she'd be fine for the rest of the walk, so I lit my cigar. Unbidden, she l took my right hand. With the panatela cigar nestled in the corner of my mouth, I had my one hand available to take her left.

Sarah and I walked mostly in silence, warmed by our heavy coats. Traversing the park, we followed the bends of Bull Creek as it moved north until it touched Osage above the park. I was into my second cigar by now, and Sarah had just finished her bowl. Stopping at the corner of Osage, with practiced hands, she inverted the bowl and tapped the remaining loose ash out. I watched the ash scatter from her palm with the first gust of wind.

Walking back, we stopped back into Howards for chill-cutting hot coffees. My watch told me it was a quarter past three. Our coffees finished, I walked her home to the ladies' campus residence. At the perimeter gate, she turned and beckoned me to bend down closer. When I did, she whispered a soft, "Thank you for lunch," and kissed my cheek. And then she went through the gate.

* * *

In the next six weeks, Sarah and I found a comfortable routine. Afternoon visits at Maul's (now for coffee or hot chocolate) and Saturday lunches at Howards. Sundays we attended the Plum Creek Methodist ten o'clock morning service with me as her escort from the Normal School fence to church and back.

We shared a smoke, talked about our lives, hopes and dreams, and eventually ended up back at the stage depot. There we shared a Sunday dinner with Hercules and Bessie Belcher, as guests at the Belcher table. Sarah was color blind in the extreme and oblivious to job titles or hierarchy. In short, she was a perfect dinner guest.

As year's end approached, my blessings continued to increase. Bessie and Hercules invited us to attend Christmas Eve services with them at the St. James African Methodist Church. We rode together with the Belcher family in their carriage. Hercules and his two sons had decorated the carriage with boughs of evergreen and holly. Buttercup, their mule, was also adorned with a crown and cascades of strung popcorn and holly berries.

After the service, back at the depot, Bessie served us all hot spiced wine, sweetened with brown sugar and redolent with the tastes and smells of cinnamon, clove and allspice. It was wonderful, except for the absence of a little medicinal brandy. When all cups were empty, Bessie announced that they were going to bed. Hercules signaled his agreement and departed the room, "to give you young folks some time to yourselves."

* * *

"Seeing that we are finally alone, can I smoke?" asked Sarah. Much as I wanted to say yes, I knew Bessie didn't permit smoking in her kitchen. Bessie believed it to be a vile habit and a sure road to hell. "Not here, Bessie's rule, but you could smoke in my room, if you would be comfortable being alone with me there?"

"Oh, I'll risk it. Lead on Mr. Finch."

After the short walk down the hall, Sarah stopped by her coat, hanging on a hallway hook. She removed a purse from a large exterior coat pocket.

I entered the dark room. She stood in the doorway while I lit the first of my three oil lamps. She took one step inside and looked around, taking the measure of the place and its furnishings.

"Please take the wing-back," I said. "I like the desk chair."

I was still standing when she sat and began to fill her pipe. "Excuse me while I go down the hall for a pitcher of water."

When I returned, she had lit her pipe.

She smiled when I placed the blue and white patterned Delft pitcher next to its matching basin. "May I make myself more comfortable, sir?"

When I nodded, she kicked off her shoes and undid the top two buttons of her white blouse.

I watched. This was a Sarah that I'd not seen before.

"Aren't you going to join me?" she asked.

144

I removed a cigar from the desk, opened the window a modest one inch and closed its curtains. I lit my cigar and sat down in the straight-backed chair.

She took the pipe from her mouth and cupped the bowl in her right hand. My eyes focused on her as she began caressing the pipe stem in long strokes. The stem moved to her lips and the warm smoke filled her mouth.

She had my undivided attention. *Is she doing that on purpose?*

Her eyes met mine.

She is!

I unbuttoned the top button on my shirt. She raised her leg and set it across my thigh. "I'm still hot. Would you help a lady off with her stockings, kind sir?"

My eyes had not left hers as she pulled the hem of her skirt up, slowly, ever higher until the leg clips of a black garter belt came into view. Neither of us looked away. I unbuttoned another two buttons on her blouse, exposing the first glimpses of the lace and skin waiting beneath.

When my hand went to her leg, she softly inhaled and blinked her eyes. Her breathing changed, and she whispered a soft, "Please."

Our moves became quicker. I ran my hand up her thigh and undid the two garter clips. Then she moved the other leg to my lap and again my hand moved up her leg.

"Please keep one lamp on while I get ready," she said.

Rising from the chair, I attended to the lamps and locked the door. When I turned back, her blouse was unbuttoned. I gently slipped it from her shoulders and let it fall onto the floor.

I wanted to be in charge, up to a point at least, so I stepped closer and began unbuttoning my shirt. It fell to the floor at my feet. Now I could hear the change in her breathing, as I lifted the silk camisole over her head, and held it before me. I smiled and dropped the silk. And my heart was pounding in my ears as I stepped out of my underwear.

She stepped closer and guided my hand to between the warm, wet folds of her body and what waited beneath. A gasp escaped her lips. I stopped my gentle touch and pulled her tight.

"My arm?" Would finally seeing or touching my inescapable loss break the magic of the moment?

It didn't. She raised up on her toes and whispered a reassuring "shuuu.u..u" as a mother might comfort a child. But with my erection pressed against her body, she had no motherly intent. And I led her to my bed.

27. Advance of the Railroads

Paola, Kansas, 1869 into 1870

I'd found a woman not put off by my arm. For so long, my fears of rejection had caused me to avoid trying to find a relationship. But now, to be no less a man in Sarah's eyes added so much joy and so many possibilities to my future. I'd found a woman that I loved and who loved me in return.

On all fronts, my life evolved in ways that pleased me. I was now Junior Warden in the line of officers in our Masonic lodge. Our GAR Post attracted new members. At the national level, the GAR began making itself known in the halls of Congress.

Back in 1862, Lincoln had promised widows they would not be left destitute, and a monthly pension of $8, plus $2 more per dependent child, was enacted. Improving the widows' pension and securing pensions for disabled veterans were two of the issues I hoped the GAR would address straight away. Perhaps in response to or recognition of the GAR founding, in 1866 Congress increased my disability pension to $20 per month.

At work, little things arose daily, such as creating signage advising travelers on the best types of clothing to wear during a coach ride. Calico and ginghams were suggested for ladies, along with veils to keep out the dust. For men, it was bandanas for dust and preferably work clothes for the trip. Warm wear in winter and always a jacket for the cool mornings. With our roads still a developing system, male passengers were often invited to help free a wheel from mud or sand.

My responsibilities at the stage depot steadily increased as I became exposed to more aspects of the job. Woodrow was introducing me to the intricacies of scheduling. I thought about it as juggling. Scheduling in supplies to the relay stations involved timing their delivery for the requested item, along with the regular delivery of food for men and animals. So, we had to order items that might be requested, such as harness, from our suppliers in advance. Easy, yes? No!

An order for replacement harness had to be made far enough in advance that things could be manufactured for our supplier, who was often a simple jobber. Jobbers bought and sold goods as middlemen between maker and end user. And don't forget to add the necessary shipping time: from manufacturer to jobbers, then jobber to me and finally, me to our relay station.

Now do this for hay, harness, horses and on down the entire alphabet of moving parts. "A" is for ammunition. "B" is for buffalo robes or blankets and on and on through "W" as in wagon wheels. Easy, huh?

* * *

In anticipation of May 30th, I convinced the membership of the GAR Post to mark the day with a 'Decoration Day' parade down our main street. Our post namesake Col. McCaslin had passed away, late last year. Our new post commander, Warren Smiley, enthusiastically agreed. So, our members hunted up any and all parts of their uniforms and marched in formation under Capt. Smiley's leadership, on this first Decoration Day.

Then on May 10, 1869, my long-held fears about the arrival of rails came into sharp focus. The picture on the front page of the Miami County Republican showed locomotives of the Central Pacific and Union Pacific railroads nose to nose at Promontory Point, Utah. The final spike being driven was supposed to be of pure gold. Rails now connected our country from coast to coast.

No one said it, but I doubted I was alone in seeing either the beginning of the end for our industry or the foreshadowing of great change. If we evolved, we could survive. But I believed that to fight the iron giants and their steel webs was a sure path to destruction.

Our first concession came in January 1870, when our northern terminus moved south from Kansas to the newly established railroad town of Kit Carson, Colorado. And the steel storm was just beginning.

In May 1870, Brad and Jared saw the area where their stage line was likely to remain economically viable: Southern Colorado, along the Santa Fe trail into the New Mexico territory and west through the tiny town of Las Vegas and on over Tehachapi Pass into California.

Mac Foster, one of our best drivers, and I set out in a two-mule buggy to lay out a new route. We left the old stage route at the Iron Springs relay station and crossed over to Bent Canyon on the Purgatoire River. We'd open a new relay station at Bent's Fort. The next night, Mac and I stayed comfortably in the Overland Hotel in Trinidad. The route we'd traversed would be easier on both passengers and our Concord Coaches.

Mac and I found a thriving community in Trinidad. Settlers were arriving daily. There was water from the Purgatoire River and high-grade coal was abundant, good enough to be made into coke to fuel steel blast furnaces. I liked what I saw, judging from the vitality of the town and because it looked to be one of the last places that our coaches would be displaced by the railroads.

Raton Pass before Stagecoach Road

The next day, we headed out and followed the southern path over the Rockies at Raton Pass. Dick Wootton and his partner, George C. McBride, had built a 27-mile-long toll road over the pass. They charged $1.25 per wagon, 25 cents per horseman, and a nickel per animal. Indians were never charged. Raton Pass was still not a place for the inexperienced. The banks of the road were littered with broken parts of wagons that didn't make it. Sometimes in winter, it took up to seven days to complete the crossing.

We laid out a new route that minimized some of the steep sections, trading distance for comfort and speed. We had more winding turns but never with more than a gentle three and a half percent grade, all the way over the Raton summit at 7,800 feet. Once over the pass at Raton, New Mexico, we were only 180 miles northeast of Santa Fe, the territorial capital.

Raton Pass with Stagecoach Road

And no sooner had we arrived back at Paola than the storm of railroad expansion arrived. On June 21, 1870, the Denver Pacific Railroad reached Denver from the Union Pacific mainline at Cheyenne, Wyoming. On August 15th, the Kansas Pacific Railroad came into Denver from Kansas City, Missouri.

* * *

I saw two immediate questions that needed answering. First and most important, would Sarah Fain be my wife? God, I hoped so. Secondly, would the company give me the job of Station Agent at Trinidad, when H.B. Smith, our current agent, retired in the spring?

I picked the spot and the time to ask Sarah. I needed privacy to ask the biggest question of my life. Facing shot and shell had held no more terror than this. I'd rather face the guns again than a simple 'No' from Sarah. But now was the time and there was no going back. So, I picked a time and place. But it took me days to do it, as I wrestled with my own self-doubt.

What do I do if she says no?

I'll ask the bosses for another station, so I won't have to look at her every damn day.

"Sarah, how would you like a buggy ride out to the river after church next Sunday? I have some news, about my job that I want to share. And I need your help with some big questions."

The August days are always hot, so I chose an early evening ride. "The birds should be active and maybe the fish are jumping. Let's go see." As always, Sarah sat on my right as we rode together on the carriage seat. I stopped at our favorite promontory above the Marais des Cygnes River.

"This is beautiful Duane, what a nice idea."

Now or never. And all of my rehearsing vanished. Shit!

I secured the reins to a metal hook on the kickboard and took my darling's hand.

"Sarah, will you marry me?" And I breathed a sigh of relief at just getting the words out. The seconds seemed like minutes as her mouth opened ever so slightly and her eyes locked on mine. Then her bow mouth morphed into a smile. But she didn't speak and her even momentary silence dragged on.

"Say that again, please, Mr. Finch."

I realized I was holding my breath. I'm pretty sure my face had gone from pink to red by then, as I exhaled loudly and refocused myself.

"Will you marry me?" *Please, please, please!*

"You are a kind man, a gentle and considerate lover."

Oh-oh, here it comes… 'I like you as a friend.'

Then she said YES!

I left the details of the wedding to her, giving help only when asked. All I wanted was to please and protect this woman who'd accepted my heart when offered and now gave hers to me in return. Oh, and I even remembered to tell her about getting the job in Trinidad.

On September 11, we sealed our vows at the altar in our Plum Creek Methodist Church. The church was filled with my friends, Sarah's friends from the college, and our congregation. Distance and health issues prevented either set of our parents from attending the wedding. Bradley Barlow, Jared Sanderson and their wives attended the ceremony. Their wedding presents to us were one hundred dollars and a promise that the Trinidad station would be mine. Sarah and I moved to a rented house on West Osage Street in Paola.

Life was good and the new Mrs. Finch set about furnishing our little home. Wedding presents of linens came from her colleagues and students. Mrs. Belcher did a pruning of her kitchen for pots, pans, dishes and utensils that she could do without. Congregants from Plum Creek Methodist arrived with bits of furniture. Nothing matched, but everything worked. Our only new item came from Woodrow and his wife: a new bed and mattress. "Duane, a man needs a good work bench. Use it well, my boy."

28. New Wife, New Job, New Town

Trinidad, Colorado, Spring 1871-1872

My promotion to station manager came with a raise in pay. Our marriage cancelled Sarah's widow's pension, but neither of us cared about what it cost, only what we gained.

We arrived in Trinidad on the first of April. My office occupied a corner on the ground floor of the Overland Hotel on the Main street. With the permission of my bosses, I agreed to allow Wells Fargo to operate out of our office for a reasonable monthly consideration.

First, I wanted to understand every bit of the Trinidad operation and not simply make purposeless changes to show off my authority. My first acts were to make sure our coaches were always clean, the passenger seating always comfortable, the upholstery in good condition.

Wool blankets and buffalo robes were in every coach. I added an express baggage option at just thirty cents per pound for sending small items. If you needed freight shipped, we could arrange that too. We were there to be the traveler's friend and helper.

I sent the bosses a copy of an article in the Pueblo paper, the Colorado Chieftain. The headline read "A Model Stage Line," and described the comfort of our coaches, friendliness of our drivers and beauty of our horses.

"The Barlow and Sanderson stage line cannot be surpassed for the excellence of our coaches. Everything that can be thought of for the comfort of passengers is there. And crossing the Great Divide over Raton Pass, if passengers become too warm, they can blame it on their using too many buffalo robes and blankets (sic)." The story got picked up and repeated in the Denver paper, much to our delight.

I found Trinity Masonic Lodge # 28 A.F. & A. M. on east Main Street and moved my membership from Paola to my new home. I liked where we were, and Sarah began looking for a house. We found one to her liking in town and I made a deal with the owner to rent the place.

I moved my membership from Paola to the GAR Post # 25 at Trinidad. The post already had plans for their Decoration Day celebration on May 30th. I wanted to be part of the Day of Remembrance for as long as I remained in Trinidad. With our membership now at almost thirty thousand nationally, politicians began to listen to the voice of veterans. In late 1872, the Veterans Disability Program got rewritten and my disability benefit rose to $31.25 per month.

* * *

Now I absolutely needed a gun, but the army Colt pistol I'd been given before Atlanta was no longer an option for me now. It was too big and heavy to be carried concealed. I had no desire to carry a visible pistol and holster. I needed to find a gun shop and speak to someone who knew guns.

I found the shop in town, the Roberts Gun Emporium. Greg Roberts, the owner, listened to what I wanted and, noting my disability, immediately showed me his recommendation. We were on a first name basis by then, and I watched and listened as he explained his recommendation.

"Duane, this is a Smith and Wesson Army Model 3, in .44 caliber. Revolvers only give you six shots, so for you, reloading could be a problem."

Then Greg demonstrated and narrated what his right hand could do that made this a good choice for my needs. "My thumb is pushing up on the top cylinder release." The pistol broke open from the top, just behind the cartridge cylinder. Next, Greg rotated the gun in his hand until the cylinder was inverted. I watched as the six cartridges dropped out.

"Now, I'm going to close the cylinder and repeat what you just saw, using only my right hand. Then, I'll reload it with one hand. Watch closely and then we'll see if you can do it."

The pistol barrel opened, and he dumped the cartridge cases before moving it to his left armpit. Now he inserted fresh rounds into the six cylinder chambers, one at a time, and snapped the gun closed. Smiling now, he handed the pistol to me.

"You won't be as fast reloading as I am, but you will get the job done. Your extra cartridges will be in a pocket. So, now it's your turn." I repeated the moves I'd just seen, emptying spent cartridges and reloading six new rounds. It was slow, but I could do it, one handed. *And I only dropped a cartridge once, the first time through!*

I'd practice like my very life depended on it, which someday it might.

* * *

Indian problems erupted in September of '71, so I encouraged every male passenger to travel armed. None of our coaches were molested beyond the occasional band of young bucks who menaced us by charging and withdrawing without firing an arrow or gun. This we came to refer to as "Indian Tag."

Then one of our drivers claimed that forty Indians had killed Myron Higbee, just miles from town. But the other employee riding in the driver's box told me it hadn't happened. We needed to go up there and find out the truth.

I joined a posse of forty men, and we cornered a band of Cheyenne and Arapahoe in a canyon. We were all armed, myself with my newly purchased Smith and Wesson pistol. I could hit where I aimed.

The posse wanted to attack, but I had my doubts. The men I had to kill in the war were too fresh in my recollection. Instead, I held up an improvised white flag and ventured out to parley with the Indians.

They were starving and just trying to feed their families. They had done nothing more threatening than raid Myron Higbee's watermelon patch. I made a deal with their leader, Hokecii, to provide two steers to his band, at company expense.

"Will you leave in peace if I do that?" Hokecii took me at my word and agreed. A very much alive Myron Higbee began picking melons and presenting them to women in Hokecii's band.

I was happy to play peacemaker, to talk and listen rather than fight. Then word came to the posse from a scout that another 200 Indians were headed our way.

Oh shit! The forty of us are no match for 200 Indians.

155

Hokecii stepped away from his small group and stood by my side as the distant dust approached and soon revealed a large number of mounted Arapaho braves. Our 40 guns were loaded, and we took what cover we could, hoping for the best while preparing for the worst, if a fight couldn't be avoided.

Hokeccii interceded and a needless confrontation, perhaps tragedy, was averted. Maybe some small measure of trust between whites and Indians was restored. The beeves arrived at the canyon on the next afternoon. I hoped our promise being kept would be remembered.

* * *

The railroad inched closer from the New Mexico side of the Raton Pass but no further. In June of '72, the Denver and Rio Grande railroad reached Pueblo. They were drawn by the prospect of transporting coke from the southern Colorado coal field and from the coke ovens of the Colorado Coal and Iron Company. People said that coal built Trinidad.

Colorado Coal and Iron built company towns for their workers. The Colorado Supply Company out of Trinidad set up a system of company stores for each new coal town. I made sure that their freight, new miners and the mail all came and went via our coaches or wagons. As station manager, I chose not to rage against the tide of change. Instead, I opened new routes from railheads, coal camps and gold camps.

J.L. Sanderson Coach in Trinidad

Sarah was a good wife and on the 6th of August, I was by her side when she delivered our first child, Mabel Alice. Seeing the arrival of a new life filled me with hope for the future. It also brought back to mind what Dan Daniels had said so long ago, quoting Thomas Paine, about why he chose to fight right then.

"If there must be trouble, let it be in my day that
my child may have peace."

Dan understood then, as a father, what I understood now, holding baby Mabel in my arms.

Sarah stayed home now for the baby's first year, as both our lives changed to fit the new realities of parenthood. Trying to get baby Mabel to sleep at night, on our schedule instead of on hers, was a challenge. By happy accident, we found that a buggy ride worked as a sleep inducer.

We enjoyed picnics along the banks of the Purgatoire River, as it had a host of beautiful picnic spots. I borrowed a buggy from the station and a mule. I'd walk to the station on Main and return in the buggy to our place where Sarah waited with Mabel happily ensconced in her wicker carrying basket. Sarah passed over the picnic basket resting at her feet and then handed up baby Mabel.

Then she put on her wide-brimmed hat, and I helped her into the borrowed buggy.

The October day was all I could have hoped for: clear blue sky and still comfortably warm but not hot. The mule seemed to be enjoying the day as the buggy whip never left its dashboard holder in the trip out to Sarah's chosen spot on the river.

After taking Mabel from her arms, I helped her down from the buggy seat. Then I spread out a large blanket for our tablecloth. We settled under an oak tree above a small rise with the river in the distance, and the mule settled into contentedly grazing. Then I retrieved the picnic basket from our buggy and set it down beside my wife. Sarah had tucked her legs under herself and smoothed out the folds of her skirt and Mabel had already gone to sleep in her lap.

The basket contained a large mason jar full of lemonade, two china plates, another plate of fried chicken covered with a napkin, its four corners tied together to keep the chicken in place. Next came cloth napkins and finally a pie whose smell promised plum filling concealed under its golden crust.

We ate seated side by side. What small breeze there was carried the scent of prairie grass and helped keep any flying bugs away. The plate of chicken sat in front of us, and she poured lemonade into two small jars that were to be our glasses. Our conversation started with the beauty surrounding us, then to our plans, hopes and dreams.

We shared the pleasures of a smoke after a good meal. And the baby slept on.

As she loaded the used dishes back into the basket, I reclined, leaning on my elbow. Her chore done, she unfolded her legs and leaned down to rest her head on my thigh. Where she looked or what she saw, I don't know, but at some point, her eyes closed. The breeze, birds or the occasional sounds mostly covered her soft breathing.

Four hours had passed when she sniffed, turned her head, and opened her blue eyes. "I need to excuse myself sir," she said. I understood the message. As we got up, I addressed the immediate problem.

Pointing to beyond the buggy, I spoke. "Ladies on the left," then gesturing toward the river; "men on the right?" She gave a prim nod, and we both stepped away to answer nature's call. After finishing my duty, I waited at our blanket for Sarah's return. Mabel had come awake and fussed for attention.

Sarah calmed our baby with her breast. We had no words for a long while. I thought it was a sign of our deep and abiding love that sometimes nothing needed to be said. Just being together, doing nothing, was a joy.

I said we should probably start back in, so we loaded up the buggy and headed home. Sarah sat closer by my side, with the reins in my one good hand and Mabel in her wicker cradle, safe between our feet.

Life was good.

In June 1875 our second babe, whom we named Minnie Stella, appeared. Neither of the girls was tagged with their Grandfather's penchant for double initials.

Two more lines came into Colorado in 1873. By 1876, when President Grant welcomed us into the Union as the 38th state, eight more railroad lines had extended themselves into what was once stagecoach country.

What was good for Colorado was damn sure not good for me. The railroads would put us out of business. It was just a matter of when, not if, and what could we do to forestall the inevitable?

In April 1876, the Denver and Rio Grande railroad reached El Moro, just four miles outside Trinidad. Our town was hungry for a rail line that would move coal from the rich coal fields just to our south. The coming of the rail was the harbinger of business. The population tripled as the mercantile class found ready markets for their wares. I watched the engine of commerce replace wooden shops with multistory brick and stone businesses. We became the economic center of southern Colorado, the gateway to the riches of coal and Leadville gold.

Trinidad's economic boom gave rise to regional start-up stage lines. Now our competition was not just from rails, but also from smaller outfits. They had cheaper fares and more daily runs from one point to another. These small competitors could offer lower fares by focusing on small routes that didn't require the infrastructure that Barlow and Sanderson needed.

We had a small lifeline tossed by the US Post Office in 1877. Our contract for mail delivery to Las Animas County towns was increased from triweekly to daily. Every bit helped.

* * *

In September 1878, I had the pleasure of taking former Union General Lew Wallace from the El Moro railhead to Santa Fe. General Wallace had been appointed Territorial Governor of New Mexico by President Hayes.

The general and I rode alone in one of our two-wheel buggies, pulled by a two-mule team. I knew he had commanded a large part of The Army of Tennessee. He'd been involved with the taking of Fort Donelson and had failed in a rescue effort at Shiloh.

He was profoundly affected by the war and had turned to politics. He was beginning a long-held dream, writing a book. It would be something that celebrated his strong Christian faith. It was to be called "Ben-Hur: A Tale of the Christ."

* * *

The tide of rails was unstoppable and in 1878, the Atchison, Topeka and Santa Fe railroad completed the four-mile connection to Trinidad and then on and over Raton Pass. Now our days as a major transportation medium were truly numbered.

Our business to Leadville was lost to the railroad. My boss, Bradley Barlow, sold out to Jared Sanderson. I supervised closing our Trinidad station and arranged the sale of our stock, freight wagons and routes to Wells Fargo. The Overland stage was done and so was my job. The company came to its end in January 1880 when the last of their livestock and rolling stock was sold off.

While Sarah stayed in Trinidad with our two girls, my connections helped me get on with a regional stage line over the pass in the New Mexico Territory. She had long ago traded her career as a teacher for the harder job of being a parent, God bless her. That we were known in Trinidad to the merchant community and owned our house, both helped. I knew that my brothers from the lodge and the GAR post would be there if assistance was needed. But none of this absolved me from having left her alone. I sure as hell didn't like it, but I guess things happen that way.

Beyond the 'what if's' in my mind, I missed my wife. The first two weeks away were the hardest, just plain homesick or lovesick: some damn kind of sick, anyway. But it was hard to keep doing what needed to be done.

At the end of July 1879, I drove the final stagecoach from Otero County to Las Vegas. We arrived, and I witnessed the first train from Santa Fe that rolled in the very next day.

Catholic Hospital: Nuns Working as Nurses.

29. My Next Chapter Begins.

1879-1882

Trinidad thrived on the new rail connection to the big cities and industry of the East. The quality of life improved as we established our own water system and public school for the city.

I needed a new job. With a wife and two little girls at home, that was our immediate requirement. It never hurts to be involved with your town when looking for work. So, I founded and became foreman of our first volunteer fire company.

The Catholic Sisters of Charity established a school and a hospital. Our Jewish community opened a school and a temple for their worship. We had an opera house that played host to star performers from the East Coast. To my delight, we had two breweries and a cigar company. One branch of Charles Goodnight's famous Goodnight trail brought cattle to the Trinidad railhead.

I must have done something right in my time with the stage company because friends and even strangers were offering suggestions and opportunities. I was now running a feed lot for Charlie Goodnight and Oliver Loving's cattle. I'd get them fattened up before we put them on the train here at the Trinidad railhead. They came up from Fort Sumner along the stage route, joining their herds with John Chisum's. That job didn't last awfully long, as the cattle drives fell victim to the railroads just like the stage line had.

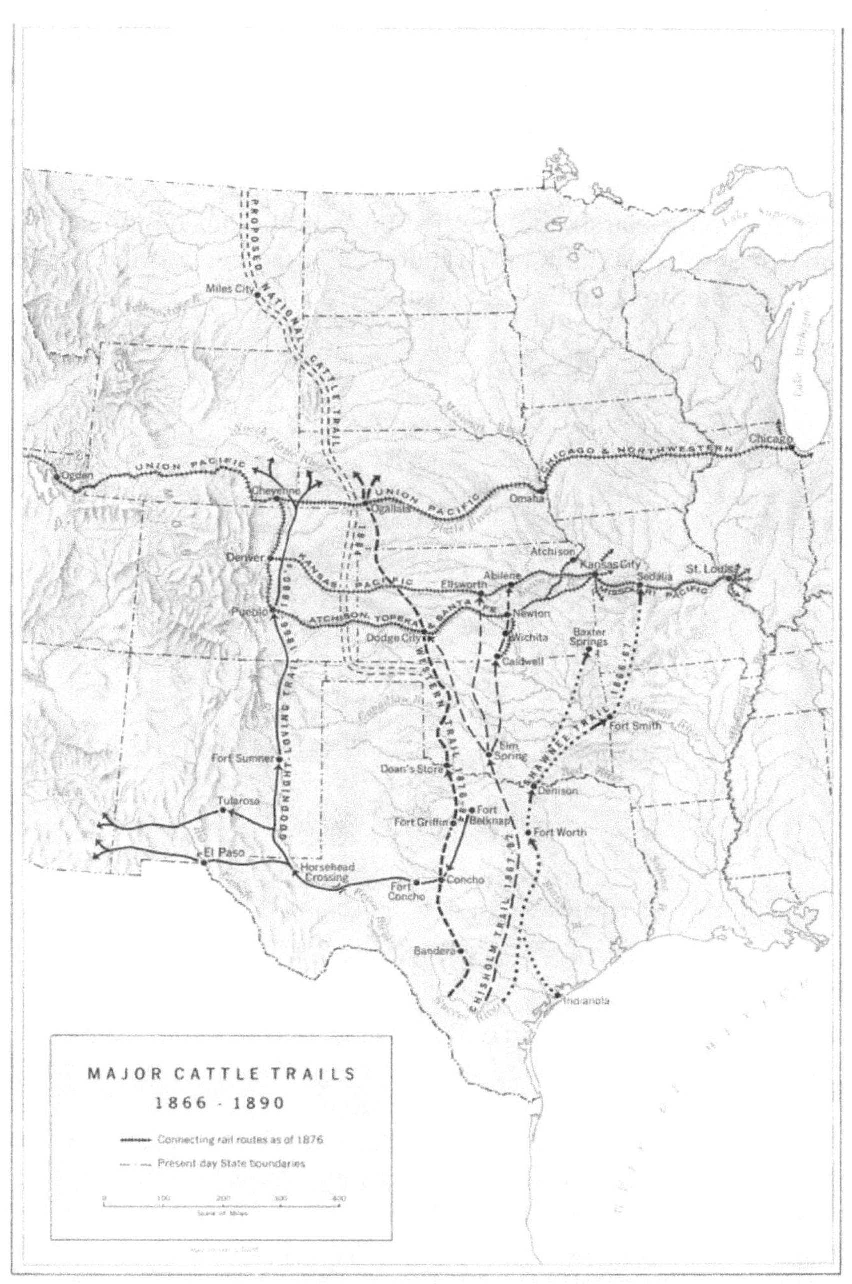

Goodnight Cattle Drive Trail

165

So, once again, I needed a job. Friends from the lodge, the GAR, and our neighbors put me up to be the city treasurer for Trinidad. I never decided if they figured I was too honest to steal, or too dumb. And I never asked.

With a steady job and a third child on the way, we needed a bigger house. Sarah and I settled on building our house and it was to be out of brick, a first for Trinidad. I purchased an empty lot over on Second Street and work began.

In June 1882, our third child, Maude Devee, arrived. Seven-year-old Minnie and big sister Mabel were thrilled. They now had a real live baby doll to help their mother attend.

I am ashamed to admit that I did not tell my wife how much I loved her every single day. I spent a long time not believing that any woman, let alone one as beautiful as my Sarah, could love a one-armed reprobate like me. Those were some lonely times, I'll tell you. It was wonderful to sit at our table and not be "the gimp."

In April 1882, our mayor appointed a city marshal. *Why? When we already have a police department?* I think the mayor had read one too many dime novels.

I added him to the payroll at seventy-five dollars per month. His name was Bartholomew Masterson, but he preferred "Bat." He was well known as an army scout for General Nelson Miles, and as the onetime marshal of Dodge City, Kansas.

How he found his way to Trinidad, I'll never know. He brought with him a volunteer deputy, Wyatt Earp. Earp didn't stay for long. His reason for coming at all seemed to be talking Marshal Masterson into helping keep another gambler, Doc Holliday, from being extradited from Colorado back to Arizona. Masterson pulled it off and Earp departed.

Marshal Masterson had a lucrative part-time job. He dealt Faro every night in our largest saloon and card parlor. When Bat ran for election, he lost badly. Our local paper summed it up nicely. "There are now two bankers running for city offices, Mr. Taylor of the Las Animas County Bank and Mr. Masterson of the bank of 'Fair O.' Both have a large number of depositors. One holds the depositor's money and the other receives his deposits for keeps." Masterson's brief career in Trinidad ended in April of 1893.

Bat Masterson

30. The Stonewall War

1876-1888

Two of my friends, Dick Russell and Lucien Maxwell, had been
fighting since 1875 about who owned what piece of dirt on the upper

Purgatoire River drainage. There were enough folks out there in what they called Stonewall to build a school and a church. I did business with these two idiots. We ran a short line stage out there and hauled freight out to Dick's store, and he became postmaster.

Russell Homestead at Stonewall

Lucien bought from Dick's store and our wagon brought into town all the produce, feed and grain that came out of the Stonewall Valley. If I got either of them alone for a friendly drink or three, they were perfectly decent fellas. But put 'em together, and it was like two cats fighting in a bag.

Anyhow, somewhere along the line, Lucien formed the Maxwell Land Grant and Railroad Company. That sure has a nice ring to it, doesn't it? Even if there's no railroad. Dick and his friends had patent deeds to their homesteads. It's a damn shame that the two of them couldn't just get along.

In 1888, I was elected a County Commissioner for Las Animas County and helped form the Trinidad Chamber of Commerce. By this time, Lucien had sold his original 96,000 acres to a foreign syndicate. These foreigners claimed they owned damn near the whole of the Purgatoire River valley.

Settlers who had homesteaded parts of an old Mexican landgrant where they had been invited and encouraged to settle came in conflict with corporate interests. Legal governance, in the form of recorded deeds, replaced the homesteaders' rights of occupancy. Conflict between the Old West and the New erupted.

Now the owners hired a fella named Pels to manage the property. Pels told the Stonewall settlers in the valley that their deeds were no good. They were squatters. But old Pels said he'd be nice. He'd let them all stay, if they sign over all their property and livestock to the company and begin paying rent

Dick Russell told Pels to go pound salt up his ass and Pels swore out a complaint claiming Dick stole company cattle and timber. But Dick was acquitted by the jury. Pels backed off and told all the folks out in Stonewall they could keep their cattle, but had to pay pasture rent.

That offer went over like a turd in a punch bowl, and the foreign owners began sending out eviction notices. Things were getting worse by the day. The Stonewall folks got together and elected Dick Russell as their leader and spokesman.

Around about then, the owners built themselves a sixteen-room resort hotel for rich visitors. Between the locals, Pels and his hotel, we had a slow-moving war. Every time anyone could cause the hotel a problem, like on deliveries, unexplained water problems or groups of folks hanging around outside, they did. The valley folks let Pels' guys know how welcome they were: not very.

Finally, the county Sheriff sent six deputies out to the hotel to keep the peace, and the land company rounded up thirty-five hired guys. Russell formed his own posse of two hundred locals. Fifty of them, masked and armed, headed for the hotel.

Dick Russell came out under a white flag of truce and told the deputies to leave. Then shooting started. Dick and one settler got shot. They were trading shots for an hour before somebody held up another white flag and things slowed down, but didn't stop. The barn behind the hotel got torched. All hell was breaking loose.

About that time, a rider from Stonewall come into town and straight to my house.

Sixteen-year-old Mabel answered the knock on our door.

"Child, you need to get your Father."

"Dad, it's for you," she called, a note of panic clear to my ear. Something about the man at our door had scared her. Coming through the house, I saw George Smith, our mayor's assistant, and from his fidgeting and facial expression, he was agitated.

"Mr. Finch, you need to come." I detected panic in his voice.

What's going on?

"There's a mob of armed ranchers out at Stonewall and they seem dead set on dealing some rough justice to the Maxwell syndicate. They've got six deputies holed up in the hotel. Dick Russell's been shot, and a Mexican boy killed. Mayor Bedke thinks both sides will listen to you," and he paused to catch his breath.

Ah shit, I knew that someday this would happen.

"Tell the mayor I'll head out there and try to tamp things down. Now, I want you to get over to Dick Wootton's place. Tell him what you told me. Ask him to meet me at Hunter's Livery Stable."

* * *

"Sarah," I called out. "I have to go. There's trouble out at Stonewall, I'll be back. Don't wait dinner."

I found my fellow County Commissioner already at the stable. We decided it was time for us to go talk some sense into these Hoople-heads.

Wootton and I took a buggy out to the hotel. It was empty. The deputies had escaped, but more settlers had arrived. There were four or five hundred armed gunmen, looking to settle up with Pels. That night, when Dick Russell died from a deputy's bullet, the hotel was burned. So there we were with two dead, five hundred pissed off locals, and thirty-five gunmen headed our way.

"Dick, I'm going to see if I can find Pels," I said, removing my coat. I wanted both sides to know that I came unarmed and was not a threat.

I pulled Pels aside and we had ourselves a 'Come to Jesus' conversation.

"You are gonna get a lot of people killed here," I told him. "The settlers are ready to fight. Die if they have to. If that happens, you and your bosses, whoever they are, will never have a minute's peace."

"Listen here sir, the Colorado Supreme Court gave us title to the land. They are squatters, thieves. Mr. Finch, you have a reputation as an honest man; a man of your word, and of the law."

Prissy bastard.

Then Pels stopped, perhaps for the first time, considering the likely consequences of his position. "I've done business with you. Is there a way out of this situation?"

"Do you want me to go tell them that they're squatters and thieves? Dick Russell and the Mexican boy were under a flag of truce when one of the deputies you called out killed him." I watched a further change in Pels. He shook his head and seemed deflated by the situation.

Pulling out three cigars, I offered smokes to Pels and Wootton. As we smoked, mostly in silence, I was trying to think; *How can I end this fighting before more people die?* Finally, I offered a solution. It all depended on both sides compromising.

Pels agreed to give Marion Russell, Dick's widow and her eight kids, clear title to the eighty-acre parcel where they lived, and Dick had his store. Pels would ride out and stop the thirty-five hired guns. In exchange, I would get the settlers' army to go home and abandon their claims to the land. In exchange, Marion got her deed, and the settlers army went home. They could stay as tenants if they wanted, but the fighting had to end. Now.

Leaving Stonewall, I believed the problem to be solved. I suppose because both sides viewed me as an honest broker, no one else died that day. So it wasn't right, and it wasn't fair, but what are you going to do? Because things are the way they are. So get on with it. No one was happy, but you have to be alive to be unhappy.

But it turned out that things cooled but we were not done. Old Pels got replaced, which could have been a good thing. Time dragged on and the settlers dragged out their departure. Finally, three years later, lawyers for the Maxwell Group went into federal court and got a judgment, ordering the settlers off the disputed land.

When they refused to leave, the new Maxwell representative let me know that a posse of twenty-one US Marshals were on the way to Stonewall from Denver, to forcibly evict the settlers. I was given one last chance to intervene and perhaps avoid a bloodbath.

This time I met with Marion Russell, who spoke for all the settlers in the valley.

"Marion, I know all your people believe they are in the right. But so does Maxwell. What Maxwell is doing may be damned unfair, but it is legal, and legal is what you have to deal with."

Either she's not listening or doesn't believe me.

"What's coming your way this time is not the local law. This time it is a posse of twenty-one US Marshals. These men are hard, trained killers. You are facing the entire government now. If your people fight, they will for sure die or wind up in federal prison. You can't win this one, darlin'. Please, I'm asking. I'm begging; get your folks to leave or work out a new rent arrangement."

Her eyes had shifted from staring out towards the valley to my face. We held our eyes locked on each other, and finally she let out a deep sigh.

"All right, Duane, I'll speak to my people." She trusted me as an honest broker, so I took her at her word. Unsaid was our individual hopes we could keep our promises.

She agreed to get each and every family either to leave or reach a new deal on rent. The Maxwell representative and I met with the Chief Deputy US Marshall in Trinidad. He agreed to hold his men there and monitor the settlers' departure.

For the second time, my trust by both sides prevented a terrible fight.

31. Becoming Grandpa Duane and Sheriff Finch

Trinidad, 1891-1894

Duane Finch in 1923 at age 83. On the left, son-in-law
Frank Scott and his daughter Vivian.

Nineteen-year-old Mabel, our oldest, was being sparked up by a young photographer from Pueblo, Frank Scott. On the twenty-eighth of December, they tied the knot. They would live in Pueblo, for as long as that's where his job wanted him to be.

Frank worked for a big commercial firm out of Salt Lake City, the B.B. Chase Company. He and his assistant visited the Indian reservations, taking pictures of the Indians to sell back to them. Photographs were 'white-man's magic' to the Indians. .

Life was good for us and to top it off, Congress passed the first ever comprehensive military retirement act. An honorable retirement from military service earned the veteran a pension. The amount was based on an index of factors. Did you enlist or were you drafted? How long did you serve? Were you honorably discharged? What was your rank at retirement?

I began receiving $105 per month in addition to the separate disability pension. With the average family income being in the vicinity of $600, I was, as the saying goes: 'in tall cotton' and the 'tallest hog at the trough.'

I was now the master of Trinity Masonic Lodge and Commander of the Jacob Abernathy GAR post #25. We faithfully did our Decoration Day parades on May 30 of every year. With Mabel married and gone, my Sarah now had the sewing room that she'd wanted.

In July 1894, Mabel delivered her first child. Her Mother was there in Pueblo with her at the birth of my first grandchild, Duane Scott.

I'd never been up for any elected office in law enforcement and never wanted to. However, more and more folks were talking to me, or about me, as the man they wanted as our next Las Animas County Sheriff. There were a lot of folks out in the county who I'd met through our short line coach routes and freight routes to the coal camps. They told me it was because of my stopping the killing out in the Stonewall Valley, not once, but twice now. Well, I was thinking about it.

Anyway, as they say, I put my hat into the ring and stood for office in the November 1893 election. Now, let me say, I didn't know shit from apple butter about the law. But I knew what was right and how to treat folks. I guess that must have been enough, because I took over the Sheriff's job in January 1894.

Most of my job as sheriff had nothing to do with arresting crooks. I left that work to younger, better suited deputies. I dealt mostly with politicians and other agencies, so it was politics and handling disputes again. We served both civil papers and criminal warrants.

I was obliged to carry a pistol, which as always, I kept under my coat.

I'd been elected by folks who believed me to be fair and honest. That's not always recognized when you're a lawman. You are the face, the enforcer of rules and orders from other people. But that's the job.

Some cases, crooks or crimes are memorable. Especially when the perpetrator was someone I knew. It goes to show you never can tell.

* * *

In February 1895 I got called to the house of Rose De Bar on the west side of town. They called me because Ruth Kregger, wife of former sheriff Louis Kregger, was under arrest. Rose De Bar was an aspiring actress, known for attracting men, like bees to the sweet nectar of her blossoms. One of the bees being Lou Kregger.

Ruth Kregger had paid Rose De Bar a visit while Rose was sharing her artistic talents with Ruth's husband, Louis. Ruth arrived with a small hatchet, usually used for splitting kindling wood. It also worked equally well for splitting faces. Ms. De Bar got the blade planted in her face, which did her appearance no good at all.

Ruth was intent on bloody murder. When Ms. De Bar survived the first strike, she attempted to escape into her home with Ruth, hatchet in hand, in hot pursuit. Ruth landed several more blows to the back of Rose's head before Rose reached safety.

The location, the spattered blood that decorated the door and floor, and the hatchet told me all I needed to know.

"What the heck have you gone and done?" I asked Ruth, who was perched on a low stone wall that separated the De Bar house and sidewalk. Ruth looked just plain mad, and not at all worried as I had expected her to be.

"Ruth, I'm going to call Louis, and he'll meet you at the station."

"Hello, Duane. Is the little flower of Elm Street dead?" There was no remorse in her voice.

I was not hearing what I expected. I told her I didn't know.

"Duane, when we get back to the sheriff's office, may I please have my hatchet back? Just for a minute."

Oh my Christ! "No, you may not have your hatchet back. Now go along with my two deputies and quit talking."

My next stop was at the Sisters of Charity Hospital to check on Rose. Ms. De Bar would survive the attack, but she would never

177

whistle again. A proper hairstyle would hide the wounds to her skull, but no amount of powder, paint or even plaster would fix her face. Any damage to her brain remained an unknown.

* * *

Most of the folks that I ever arrested were ashamed of themselves, remorseful and meek as lambs. I brought back Juan Trujillo from Pueblo for trial. He was a schoolteacher and taught my two youngest girls. Juan had written bad checks and tried to mortgage somebody else's property to cover the checks.

* * *

Another time, I took Abraham Hicks into custody on an assault charge. Abe had been one of my predecessor's deputies. Hicks was a big man and quick with his fists, so I took two of my men along, but had them hold back.

I treated everybody with respect and made it clear that the accusations against them were not mine. I was just doing a job, and if not me, then somebody else would. Abe came along quietly.

* * *

In 1897, I arrested E. J. Stark, the son of a long-time friend. His Dad, Albert, was a Stonewall Valley man who I'd known since I'd come to town. Albert had been involved in the Stonewall wars with Maxwell before he started the Starkville Coal Company.

Over three hundred and seventy head of sheep had been stolen from the Troy ranch. I caught one thief and recovered all but one hundred sheep. I picked up a trail and caught E. J. loading sheep into rail cars for shipment to distant markets. Honestly, it hurt to be putting hand irons on the boy.

"God damn it, son, why the hell would you do something like this? Your family has plenty of money. You come from good stock. It's going to break your mother's heart when she hears that you're in my jail."

I kept my eyes locked on the boy, waiting for him to say something. But he didn't. After delivering the kid to jail, it needed to be me that told Albert. So, I took a buggy out to the Stark Ranch. He met me at his porch, as my dust had announced my arrival in advance. I declined his offer to come into the house and see the missus.

"Albert, I need to speak to you alone. Where can we do that?" We decided to wander over to his corral fence.

"DD, you are making me uncomfortable. What the hell is going on? Am I in some kind of trouble? Maxwell trouble again?"

I cut him off with a hand gesture. "I wish we weren't having this conversation. But, since it has to take place, best that it be with me. I arrested your boy today."

His eyes widened and blood rose in his face.

I held up an open hand. "Please, just listen. I caught him with a hundred head of sheep, stolen from the Troy ranch out by Folsom. He was loading the animals in a Gulf and Western railcar." I watched as the color drained from his face and his fists unclenched. Neither of us spoke for a long time. It gave me no joy to see my friend wilt before my eyes.

"Did the boy say anything?"

I told him no, nothing was said, neither in explanation nor excuse. "Albert, that's all I know. He's in my jail now. All I can tell you is I tracked down one of the three thieves and recovered two hundred seventy-five of the sheep. Then I followed the trail to the railhead, where I arrested the boy. What happens to him is none of my concern. That will be for the Magistrates' Court." With Stark still in shocked silence, I decided I should go.

As I turned to leave, Albert spoke. "Thank you for delivering the news yourself."

Mabel, Duane, Frank, and baby Phillip Scott

In May my grandson Duane Scott was taken by the Scarlet Fever. Frank was down with the fever himself, and the doctors weren't sure he would survive. We left Mabel to care for Frank with her mother there for comfort. I brought the boy's body back to Trinidad for burial. I laid him to rest in our Masonic Cemetery, where I planned to join him in eternal rest when the Lord called me home.

Duane Scott's Headstone in Trinidad

In July 1899 I had my last big case in the middle of that bad year for our family. The Ketchum Gang—Thomas, who called himself Black Jack, along with his brother Samuel and an ever-changing cast from the 'Hole in the Wall Gang'— took to robbing trains. They stole a large payroll off an Atchison, Topeka and Santa Fe train traveling to Deming, New Mexico over Raton Pass. The gang robbed trains just over the territorial line southeast of Las Animas County.

I was part of a posse. Ed Farr, sheriff of neighboring Huerfano County and five of his men, joined with me and five of my deputies. Bill Reno, a railroad detective, tracked the gang into a canyon just over Raton Pass. We shot it out with them.

Going in, it was clear to us all that people were likely to die that day, and we didn't want it to be any of us. Black Jack, his brother Sam and their gang were cornered in a box canyon. There was no way out except through us. There were six of them and thirteen of us, so Ed and I put our heads together and came up with a plan.

Waiting them out would take days. Charging into their guns was a fool's errand and I'd already done that once in my life. So, we had to outthink 'em. I told my idea to Sheriff Ed.

"What say, we have half our men keep em' pinned down from here. We've got good cover right where we are. Then you, with those two good arms, take two men and see if you can get to the canyon rim and maybe have an angle on them from above? We'll send three up the other side of the canyon, so we've got them from the front, sides, and above." I waited as Ed thought on it for a minute.

"I like it, DD. They either have to fight in three directions at once or leave their cover and come out for a face-to-face. Where they are now, they'll use their rifles, but if they make a break for it then it's gonna be their pistols, moving and firing, against our rifles from cover." And so we did, while we still had the light.

Ed and his five deputies took off for the canyon rim. They'd shoot as soon as anyone had a target. My men and Bill Reno stayed put. Each of my five was given a field of fire for their Winchester "yellow boys." The fields of fire overlapped just like I'd set up my men during the war. Bill and I were the sergeants, backing up their line where needed. I was using experience I hoped I'd never have to rely on again, but I was glad to have it.

An hour later, someone started firing down from above, and the battle was on. Their gang's cover had been between them and us. We sure as hell surprised them, and the smell of black powder smoke that I'd learned to hate filled the air again. Our men were lying prone and ready, but they held their fire until there was a target. I took cover behind a big pine, my .44 in hand.

When the gang broke from cover only four came out. Our line was ready as the four rode out together in a bunch, and all our guns opened up on them. One of our bullets hit Sam Ketchum and dropped him from his horse. We watched the other 3 desperados get away. We had a wounded Sam, down but not out.

"Come on boys, let's finish the job," and I led my men out in a skirmish line. We moved slowly, from cover to cover as best we could, towards the spot where Ketchum had fallen. He was alive all right, because up he reared and shot me. The shot hit me in the right side. Son of a bitch, it hurt. Getting shot at fifty-six feels much worse than it did at twenty-two. But it didn't hit anything I couldn't live without.

My men had flanked his spot and when one of my deputies screwed his gun barrel into Sam's ear, the show was over. Now came the inevitable butcher's bill. One of Ed Farr's deputies was wounded.

The wounded deputy and I were taken to Raton for doctoring and later sent home from there. Bill Reno saw to it that the railroad paid the medical bills. They put me on a train at Raton and took me back to Trinidad.

Sheriff Farr and the rest of the posse continued the chase. Another gunfight took place, with Farr and one of his people killed in the fight.

They caught the Ketchum brothers. I turned over the job of taking the wounded Sam Ketchum over to my Chief Deputy, O. T. Clark.

Sam Ketchum died from blood poisoning before we could hang him.

GOOD!

Black Jack Ketchum

His brother Thomas, aka Black Jack, did get caught a year later and lived long enough to hang.

Damn good!

The world became a better place, but I had had enough of the law business. I didn't stand for re-election.

32. Lost Love

1899-1900

My conclusion, based on many years of observation and study is that women are a secretive lot. Why, I have no idea. But my not knowing why neither changes nor diminishes the accuracy of the observation.

I did not know that my darling Sarah was so terribly ill. Her ability to hide the pain and the connivance of our daughters kept the reality of her situation from me for a long time: months, I suspect.

By the time I became aware of the situation, our family doctor, Dr. Hunter, had reached the limits of his knowledge, and strong drugs didn't touch her pain. I agonized over keeping her there at home. Mabel's old room, that had become Sarah's sewing room, now became her sick room. Would it be a kindness to have her in the hospital?

In the end, our daughter Mabel left her own family, now in Denver, to tend her mother. Along with her sisters, Minnie, now Mrs. Harry Jones of Pueblo, and fifteen-year-old Maude, they tended their mother's body for her final five weeks.

I never cried out from any of my own pains. Not getting shot either time. Not giving in or giving up to a slow death in Andersonville. But by God, I cried for my Sarah's pain, because it was beyond my reach to help her or take the pain upon myself. My fate was to be a silent, helpless witness, as God humbled me to his power and my impotence.

The smells of illness and death filled the house, even as my daughters kept their mother clean. Unspoken, familial roles changed. My daughters brought me to their mother's side when they could and barred my way when they knew I shouldn't be there. God bless them all, for helping me keep my last memories of Sarah as peacefully sleeping. The end came on December nineteenth, 1899.

Mabel found me sitting on our porch, where I'd taken to waiting, far from the mingled smell inside the house. From the look on her face, a calculated mask that revealed no emotion, I knew.

"Dad, Mama's gone."

She brought me to the bedside, where we sat together. I held my bride's hand as tears fell from my unfocused eyes. Unnoticed, Mabel had faded away, leaving me the privacy and dignity to mourn alone. Finally, when Dr. Hunter arrived, summoned by Minnie, I left Sarah's side for the last time, at least in this earthly existence.

Goodbye for now, my darling. Rest in the arms of the Lord. There's no pain anymore.

* * *

With my wife of thirty years gone, I didn't cease to function or feel. I just discovered that my mourning came and went on its own time, often when I least expected it. It just came upon me and struck me down, unable to hear or to see through my tears, until it, not I, decided to pass.

Between Dr. Hunter and my many friends, Sarah was prepared for her journey at Charlie Innes's funeral home over on Main. The Masonic Cemetery prepared her grave. Reverend L. T. Hall, from the Methodist Church of Trinidad, conducted the service.

Sarah was a lifelong Baptist, so she didn't drink alcohol and we didn't dance. But other than those small things, we held the same beliefs. Nothing in Reverend Hall's reading or sermon would have been a problem for her. My eulogy for her was short, and I was lucky to complete even that.

Every member of Trinity Masonic Lodge was there at the service and the graveside. Sarah's sisters from the Eastern Star, most being Masonic wives, were there too. Our presence was shown by the ceremonial aprons worn and our ending of each prayer with our ritual phrase, "So mote it be."

As her coffin was lowered, the Reverend spoke his words of comfort.

> "We die and are buried. We are held in God's keeping. We commend to your mercy all who have died, that your will for them may be fulfilled, and we pray we may share with all your saints in your eternal kingdom."

And then she was gone, at fifty-four. Days later, I ordered her headstone. I chose one for us both. We would share the long dreamless sleep of death together, near little Duane. I couldn't show my love to either of them anymore, but I would never love them any less.

Finch Headstone

I had long ago reconciled myself with the prospect of my own death. Alone with my thoughts before many a battle, I'd come to accept that death takes us all. Only the time, place, manner and means of its arrival are unknown to us. So, thinking about joining my Sarah held no terror for me.

Death would come quick and clean. I began to pick out a place, so Maude would not discover a mess. It was so close, my .44, right there in the desk drawer. In my hand, it was a friend and a tool. We looked at one another, its one black eye staring me in the face. But not today. I had chores that I would not leave undone, so I returned my friend to its resting place and poured myself a drink.

Where was that 'soldiers joy' when I finally and truly needed it? The whisky wasn't doing the job. It didn't blank my mind or stop the waves of sorrow that washed over me. *Shit-shit-shit.* No matter how hard I tried, over those many days, nothing killed the pain.

And when I went back to the desk drawer days later, my one-eyed friend was missing.

33. Winding down

1901 and On

Eventually, the mourning of my dead wife came upon me less frequently. I needed to get on with my life and at least finish raising my daughter. Now, there's the rub. Eighteen-year-old Maude stepped into running the house. Unbidden, she knew from watching her mother what needed to be done.

Her concern reached me through multiple hugs given every day. "Don't worry Daddy, Mama taught me everything I need to know. We are going to be fine."

Have to make do until she snags some fella. Or I buy her a dog.

So I did get her, or us, a dog. I found him in our city dog pound, a reject, just like I had thought of myself, until I met my Sarah.

"Maude, his name is Easel."

"Dad, he only has three legs! Couldn't you at least have found us a normal dog? One with four legs? And he's filthy!" Then, putting her hands on her hips, she continued. "He is not coming into my clean house until he has had a bath."

God, she looks and acts just like her Mother.

"He was on sale, 25% off. The four-legged dogs were more expensive."

Easel sat at my feet. His head turned to each human as they spoke, but he otherwise remained a quiet observer. When Maude's eyes focused on Easel, his tail went into motion and his eyes locked on hers. But they both remained quiet, one in a death stare and the other, lacking words or one front leg, offered his best toothy doggy smile and wagging tail.

Easel won the contest. Maude gave up on both the dog and me, and walked off. Now, I had someone who needed me, for at least morning, noon and night walks. Maude had announced that she was now grown up and fully in charge of our household.

Maude became Mrs. Clifford Davis on July 17, 1901. Once again, change was thrust upon me.

* * *

My salvation came from filling my time with work and friends. In the evenings, I attended every meeting of our GAR post and took charge of organizing our annual Decoration Day Parade on May 30th.

Our political influence grew, as I'd long expected it would. With over seventy thousand members nationally, the GAR was a force in the elections of Presidents Hayes, Garfield and Harrison, all of whom were GAR members.

The GAR led the way in getting the national 'Universal Old Age and Disability Pension Act' passed. My disability pension increased to forty-five dollars a month, not that I cared or needed the money.

The war, the friends I'd made and those I'd lost were never far from my mind. I communicated with our national headquarters about their "monument projects." All over the former battlefields, military units from both sides were erecting memorials to where they had stood on the fateful days.

Whether history would record how our Iowa 3rd Infantry had anchored the Union line in the peach orchard at bloody Shiloh was yet to be written. But I knew what we'd done on that April morning, so long ago. I knew eleven Iowa units took part in the battle, some by my side and others back at the Hornet's Nest. I also knew that 2,400 of my companions were wounded or died there.

I gave my time and my money to help erect a monument to my brothers in arms who'd stood with me and died within my sight. Our combined efforts, coordinated through the GAR posts raised $25,000.

I was there in November 1906 at the statue's dedication. My uniform still mostly fit, 33 years after the battle.

Trinidad was now the fourth largest city in Colorado. The overlap of my connections from my work as city treasurer, the masonic lodge and the GAR kept me pleasantly busy. I filled my time with people, not possessions. I had a regular group of friends, and we shared a coffee, lunch or cocktail at least once every day.

The only fly in the ointment: I couldn't cook, didn't want to do my laundry or clean my own house. I guess I'd never realized how many things Sarah and the girls had done. Everything had always seemed to just happen naturally. But no more.

Women from the Methodist church auxiliary took it upon their themselves to "solve my problem." That I saw no difficulty didn't seem to matter to the ladies. Theirs was a solution in search of a problem. As a matter of fact, Easel did more sniffing around than me.

An unmarried, successful 59-year-old-man who was not a drunk, gambler or wife beater was an offense before God, in their minds. And it could not be allowed to stand! So, on they came as stealthy as a Confederate raider.

"DD, you should come over for Sunday dinner," said lodge brother Otis McCracken.

How could I say no?

Nola McCracken met me at the door. "Well don't you look handsome, Duane, but my gosh, have you lost some weight?"

No, I haven't.

"Duane, I want you to meet my friend Luella. She brought us a pie, made from her own apples, and I asked her to stay for dinner." What could I do but smile?

Otis, you bastard.

"My Theodore used to love my pies so. He passed last year. Nola tells me you lost your wife recently. I understand and I'm so very sorry."

I confined myself to a nodding acknowledgment. *And you want to ease my pain.*

Sweet Luella sat across from me at dinner. She had no obvious flaws. Seemed to have all her own teeth and no glass eyes. I guessed her to be somewhere on the backside of 40.

Her war paint was artfully applied and the decolletage of her dress seemed to promise much from her hidden assets. I never realized how smart I was or how my conversation sparkled until now. And so it went.

By the third, or maybe it was the fourth time that some female surprise attack happened, I became convinced that if I were a woman, well hell, I'd want to marry me. When on occasion I was offered the opportunity to engage in one of the marital prerogatives, I did dip my pen into strange ink.

* * *

Dan Taylor, our mayor, put me in touch with Mrs. Aurelio Moreno. Mrs. Moreno worked for the city. There were two older daughters who helped with the house and cooking. Her twin boys just turned eight. Socorro Moreno wanted part-time work. With Aurelio's permission, his wife became my housekeeper.

Socorro kept the house and did my laundry. She always had dinner ready for me, keeping warm in the oven. There was always the making of a breakfast, simple enough for a one-armed man to manage. It all just happened naturally.

The Moreno family came to sort of adopt me and I enjoyed many meals at Aurelio and Socorro's table. Somewhere along the line, I became 'Tio Duane'. It sounded to me like 'Da-Juan-A', but that didn't matter. I was given respect and acceptance.

The twins, José Alonso and José Benito, were named for their grandfathers. I'd just call them Jos-a and Jos-b. I'd take them fishing down on the Purgatoire. They always gave out with "ooh" when they watched how I baited my hook, and I always laughed.

I remember picking them up at their house for a day at the river. Socorro handed me a lunch bag. "José, your shoes are on the wrong feet," I said, pointing.

"They're the only feet I've got," came his defiant answer. Tio 'Da-Juan-A' or not, he would not let a perceived slight go unchallenged. Socorro's response was immediate. In rapid Spanish, she explained my meaning. About all I caught was for him not to act like a 'Macho', which I knew was a stud donkey.

After changing right shoe to right foot, I hugged the boy.

"Lo siento mi Tio, I'm so sorry," and he hugged me back.

* * *

With my life running smoothly, I had time, energy and inclination to do things bigger than myself. Mayor Taylor, The Daughters of the American Revolution, and I worked to establish a second city park. It would be called 'Kit Carson Park' in honor of Dan Taylor's departed friend and his multiple connections to Trinidad.

"I was there when we put the general to rest. He was a member of the craft," I told Dan.

To my surprise, there was some opposition to the park being named after Kit Carson.

"He did terrible things to our Indian brothers," Myra Rodgers' quote appeared in our paper. Myra and her blue hair brigade filled the city council chamber and bled all over the chamber floor about our collective sins against the Indians.

I kept my own counsel for as long as I could. "Mrs. Rodgers, ladies, you are absolutely right." And that stopped them in their tracks. There had not been a dismissal or disagreement with their heartfelt concerns.

"I will grant you that as a race, we have sinned mightily against the red man." Paused to take in the gallery of smug smiles that my comment had unleashed.

"I have personally shot at Indians, but only in defense of life or property." And I began to bend the conversation, not from the truth, but toward the whole truth. "And they have shot at me. I am glad that my actions have spared all of you from the darker sides of Indian culture. Truly, neither we nor they are universally, unfailingly nice. Both sides do what is perceived as necessary at the time.

"General Carson may have done things all of you would not do, in every case his actions were undertaken either under orders from our leaders, or in defense of your lives and your property. Will you fault him now, for doing what needed to be done?" And I paused to search the sea of faces for changes in expression.

"To deny Carson the proposed honor doesn't hurt the general or his memory. He's gone and his reputation as a hero is nationwide. But it does deprive Trinidad of an attraction that honors a former Colorado hero. Please don't deprive us of this opportunity. To show my personal support, I am here and now donating $500, to start a collection to have a statue created." Having said my piece, I sat down.

In the end we got our park and Kit Carson got a bronze statue, paid for by public subscription.

* * *

But all was not well for Las Animas County. We were 'the queen of coal country' for all Colorado, but in 1903-04, labor trouble stained the coal fields. The newly established United Mine Workers Union struck the mines, demanding better wages and safer working conditions.

This was to be our first exposure to the labor troubles that would sweep the nation. National labor leaders, including Mary Harris "Mother" Jones, came west.

In 1905, a new organization, the International Workers of the World, came into existence. Much like our Stonewall Valley trouble, the labor issues around the mines might just simmer, but it never went away. Mother Jones and the other national labor leaders were barred by the governor from entering Colorado.

* * *

In 1909, my life took a turn, at least job wise. Because of a vacancy caused by a death, I was asked to accept an appointment as Police Court Judge, until next year's election. They say that justice is blind. Well, in Trinidad, it was also crippled. I was a placeholder. My court handled the small cases, petty thefts, public intoxication, and the like.

* * *

In 1914, I became the postmaster. Another job that I had no qualifications nor experience for, except honesty, a good work ethic and appreciating other people's efforts.

Sadly, simmering labor trouble boiled over. The worst of it was at Ludlow, fourteen miles north of Trinidad. A striker's tent camp was fired on by the National Guard. The miners were resisting strike-breakers brought in by Colorado Fuel and Iron. Both miners and soldiers died in the shooting and the strikers' tent camp was set on fire. It was mostly women and children who died in the flames.

Mother Jones came back to Trinidad, defying the governor's ban. She was arrested and confined at the San Rafael Hospital, our jail being no place for a lady, even Mother Jones. But her confinement was too much.

A thousand women from all over Colorado descended on Trinidad. They marched together through the heart of town, demanding Mother Jones be released. A National Guard cavalry unit charged the women's parade, injuring many and arresting others. Mother Jones was loaded onto a train and sent out of town.

I watched as things changed from bad to worse, and federal troops arrived. Here they stayed for six months until the workers gave up their attempts to unionize the mines. I wouldn't want to be John Rockefeller or Governor Ammons on judgement day, damn their black souls.

Post Office in Trinidad

Epilogue

1930

I retired from the post office after six years, just long enough to see our new building arise. Now eighty-nine, I'm content to work in my garden and do a lot of nothing. Life is good and I'm still marching every May in our Decoration Day parade.

The winters are getting uncomfortable for my old bones and I'm closing up the house. Daughter Mabel and her Frank are now in Elko, Nevada and I'm invited there. But Elko winters are colder than here. I think I'm going to take up Harry and Minnie's offer to come out to southern California.

I'll still be back every year for Decoration Day and to see my old friends. And I do mean old.

GAR Decoration Day Reunion circa 1930. Duane Finch on the Far Right.

Duane Devee Finch left this world on October 18, 1933 after a brief illness. His body forever sleeps in Trinidad alongside his beloved wife Sarah, and near his grandson, Duane Scott.

The End

If you enjoyed this book, please do the author and other readers a favor. Go to Amazon or another online retailer and give it a review. Even a star rating would be nice.

Acknowledgements

I owe a continuing debt to my volunteer Beta readers and my consultants: Dr. Jay Hunter, M.D.; Attorney Duncan Palmatier; David Quinn; Glen Lanier; Kasse Jones; Ted Unzicker; Louise Regelin; Gary and Beverly Fuller; Lynne Whisner; Amy Johnston; Monica Ray; Monique Lillard; and Dave Gressard. I would also be lost without Gordon Long, my editor. They all struggle mightily to save me from my own literary mistakes. Also to Janis Miller, Dr. Constance Brumm, Ray and Jill Dacey, and Ted Kisha.

Special thanks to: Lt. Phil Martin of the Las Animas County Sheriff's Department for their biographical summary of Sheriff Finch.

Michael McCoy, who provided access to his copy of the Harper Weekly Journal's Annual Review of 1862.

Trinidad County Historical Society, Executive Director Ms. Emily Duren, for multiple pictures, suggestion and encouragement.

Bibliography

Beshoar, M.D., ALL ABOUT TRINIDAD AND LAS ANIMAS COUNTY, COLORADO, Trinidad Historical Society 1990, Trinidad, Colorado.

Smithsonian Institution, THE CIVIL WAR; A VISUAL HISTORY, DK Publishing 2011, New York, New York.

Snead, F. Dean, LAS ANIMAS COUNTY GHOST TOWNS AND MINING CAMPS, self-published via KDP.

Snead, F. Dean, GHOSTS OF TRINIDAD AND LOS ANIMAS COUNTY, self-published via KDP 2002.

Taylor, Morris L., First Mail West stagecoach lines on the Santa Fe trail, University of New Mexico Press, 1971, Albuquerque, New Mexico.

Afterword

What do I mean by "Historic Fiction?"

Doesn't historic mean factual, while fiction is non-factual? While both of the statements are true, they are not mutually exclusive.

My use of "historic fiction" is much more benign. I use fiction to connect historic events. History books are not about recording every aspect of events, but about summarizing history down to a manageable level. History is written by the winners. What motivated 'the bad guys?' How did things evolve as seen through the eyes of 'the losers?'

Using limited fiction allows me to elaborate on the scenes or background in which historic events took place. Examples:

In "Prisoners of War", the main characters are an interracial couple. Her internment interrupts their engagement. I explained considerably how scared our country was during the beginning of the war. How did we allow ourselves to lock away 110,000 of our countrymen for several years?

In "The Two Wars of Red Black," I created scenes based on fragments of memory my uncle recalled at age 93. One scene ties together his training to fly a particular combat aircraft. Another scene is constructed from a memory of where and why the "USAA" insurance company began.

In "Finch," history provided me with dates and places: where he enlisted and mustered in, where he fought. Based on how history recalls, his units served and fought heroically. And so it goes, but nowhere do the histories tell us how he felt.

So, I have filled in my best thoughts about the emotions. Fear, fatigue, his friends and the feeling of loss are what my fiction has added to the mix. Nothing historic has been changed, and that is how I write my historic fictions.

Sources

I started with a book titled: "Personal Military and Civil History." Prepared by the Soldiers and Sailors Historical and Benevolent Society of Washington, D.C., for Duane D. Finch. The society was founded to help veterans of our civil war. As the number of civil war survivors diminished, the organization withered away.

GAR Personal History Cover

Personal
Military and Civil History
– of –
Duane D. Finch.
Died Oct 13 – 1933

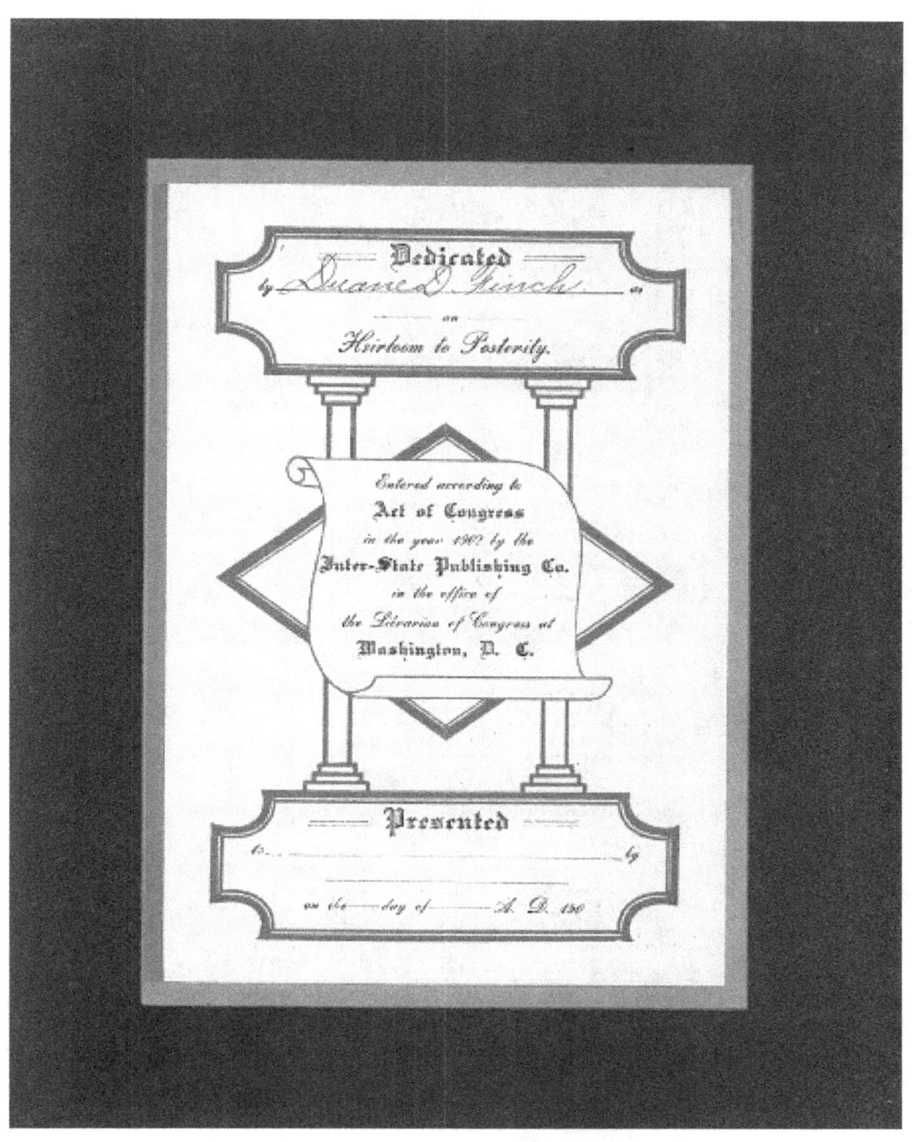

Exemplification of Providence. As approved by an act of Congress, information from the Department of the Army and printed by the Library of Congress.

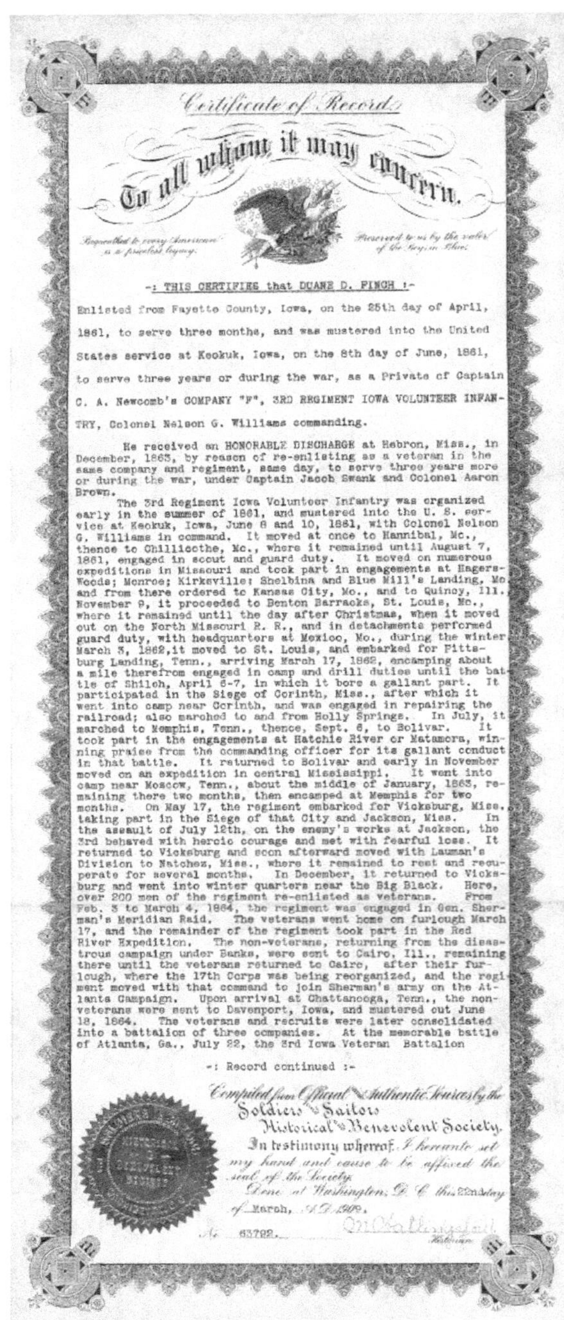

-: THIS CERTIFIES that DUANE D. FINCH :-

Enlisted from Fayette County, Iowa, on the 25th day of April, 1861, to serve three months, and was mustered into the United States service at Keokuk, Iowa, on the 8th day of June, 1861, to serve three years or during the war, as a Private of Captain C. A. Newcomb's COMPANY "F", 3RD REGIMENT IOWA VOLUNTEER INFANTRY, Colonel Nelson G. Williams commanding.

He received an HONORABLE DISCHARGE at Hebron, Miss., in December, 1863, by reason of re-enlisting as a veteran in the same company and regiment, same day, to serve three years more or during the war, under Captain Jacob Swank and Colonel Aaron Brown.

The 3rd Regiment Iowa Volunteer Infantry was organized early in the summer of 1861, and mustered into the U. S. service at Keokuk, Iowa, June 8 and 10, 1861, with Colonel Nelson G. Williams in command. It moved at once to Hannibal, Mo., thence to Chillicothe, Mo., where it remained until August 7, 1861, engaged in scout and guard duty. It moved on numerous expeditions in Missouri and took part in engagements at Hagers-Woods; Monroe; Kirksville; Shelbina and Blue Mill's Landing, Mo. and from there ordered to Kansas City, Mo., and to Quincy, Ill. November 9, it proceeded to Benton Barracks, St. Louis, Mo., where it remained until the day after Christmas, when it moved out on the North Missouri R. R., and in detachments performed guard duty, with headquarters at Mexico, Mo., during the winter. March 3, 1862, it moved to St. Louis, and embarked for Pittsburg Landing, Tenn., arriving March 17, 1862, encamping about a mile therefrom engaged in camp and drill duties until the battle of Shiloh, April 6-7, in which it bore a gallant part. It participated in the Siege of Corinth, Miss., after which it went into camp near Corinth, and was engaged in repairing the railroad; also marched to and from Holly Springs. In July, it marched to Memphis, Tenn., thence, Sept. 6, to Bolivar. It took part in the engagements at Hatchie River or Matamora, winning praise from the commanding officer for its gallant conduct in that battle. It returned to Bolivar and early in November moved on an expedition in central Mississippi. It went into camp near Moscow, Tenn., about the middle of January, 1863, remaining there two months, then encamped at Memphis for two months. On May 17, the regiment embarked for Vicksburg, Miss., taking part in the Siege of that City and Jackson, Miss. In the assault of July 12th, on the enemy's works at Jackson, the 3rd behaved with heroic courage and met with fearful loss. It returned to Vicksburg and soon afterward moved with Lauman's Division to Natchez, Miss., where it remained to rest and recuperate for several months. In December, it returned to Vicksburg and went into winter quarters near the Big Black. Here, over 200 men of the regiment re-enlisted as veterans. From Feb. 3 to March 4, 1864, the regiment was engaged in Gen. Sherman's Meridian Raid. The veterans went home on furlough March 17, and the remainder of the regiment took part in the Red River Expedition. The non-veterans, returning from the disastrous campaign under Banks, were sent to Cairo, Ill., remaining there until the veterans returned to Cairo, after their furlough, where the 17th Corps was being reorganized, and the regiment moved with that command to join Sherman's army on the Atlanta Campaign. Upon arrival at Chattanooga, Tenn., the non-veterans were sent to Davenport, Iowa, and mustered out June 18, 1864. The veterans and recruits were later consolidated into a battalion of three companies. At the memorable battle of Atlanta, Ga., July 22, the 3rd Iowa Veteran Battalion

-: Record continued :-

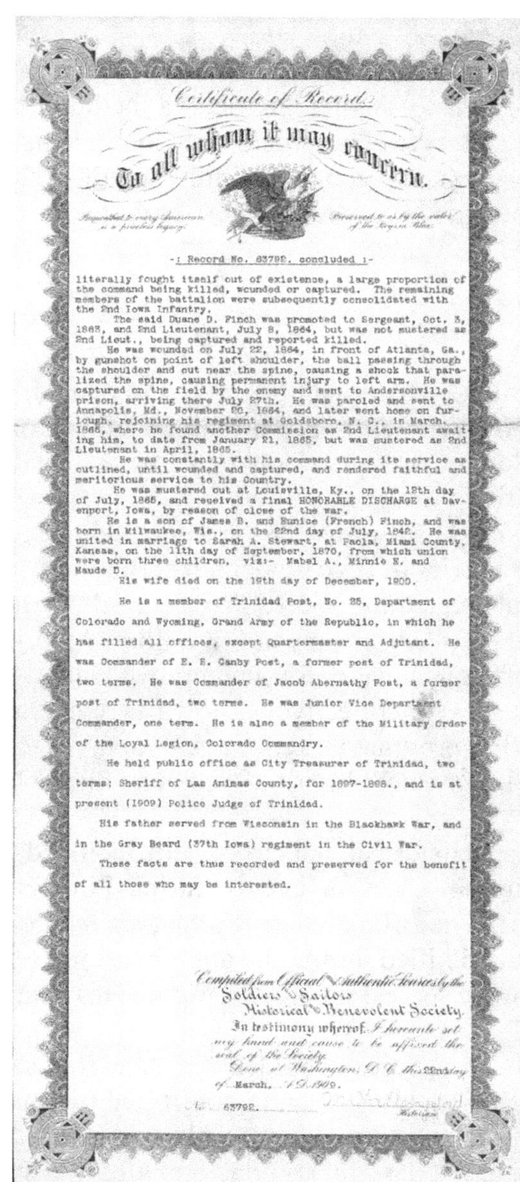

-: Record No. 83792. concluded :-

literally fought itself out of existence, a large proportion of
the command being killed, wounded or captured. The remaining
members of the battalion were subsequently consolidated with
the 2nd Iowa Infantry.

The said Duane D. Finch was promoted to Sergeant, Oct. 5,
1863, and 2nd Lieutenant, July 8, 1864, but was not mustered as
2nd Lieut., being captured and reported killed.

He was wounded on July 22, 1864, in front of Atlanta, Ga.,
by gunshot on point of left shoulder, the ball passing through
the shoulder and out near the spine, causing a shock that para-
lized the spine, causing permanent injury to left arm. He was
captured on the field by the enemy and sent to Andersonville
prison, arriving there July 27th. He was paroled and sent to
Annapolis, Md., November 26, 1864, and later went home on furlough, rejoining his regiment at Goldsboro, N. C., in March,
1865, where he found another Commission as 2nd Lieutenant awaiting him, to date from January 21, 1865, but was mustered as 2nd
Lieutenant in April, 1865.

He was constantly with his command during its service as
outlined, until wounded and captured, and rendered faithful and
meritorious service to his Country.

He was mustered out at Louisville, Ky., on the 12th day
of July, 1865, and received a final HONORABLE DISCHARGE at Davenport, Iowa, by reason of close of the war.

He is a son of James B. and Eunice (French) Finch, and was
born in Milwaukee, Wis., on the 22nd day of July, 1842. He was
united in marriage to Sarah A. Stewart, at Paola, Miami County,
Kansas, on the 11th day of September, 1870, from which union
were born three children, viz:- Mabel A., Minnie E. and
Maude D.

His wife died on the 19th day of December, 1900.

He is a member of Trinidad Post, No. 25, Department of
Colorado and Wyoming, Grand Army of the Republic, in which he
has filled all offices, except Quartermaster and Adjutant. He
was Commander of E. E. Canby Post, a former post of Trinidad,
two terms. He was Commander of Jacob Abernathy Post, a former
post of Trinidad, two terms. He was Junior Vice Department
Commander, one term. He is also a member of the Military Order
of the Loyal Legion, Colorado Commandry.

He held public office as City Treasurer of Trinidad, two
terms; Sheriff of Las Animas County, for 1897-1898., and is at
present (1909) Police Judge of Trinidad.

His father served from Wisconsin in the Blackhawk War, and
in the Gray Beard (37th Iowa) regiment in the Civil War.

These facts are thus recorded and preserved for the benefit
of all those who may be interested.

The book also contains newspaper clippings with details concerning episodes of his having been a mediator/peacemaker in land disputes and between settlers and indigenous peoples. The clippings tell a great deal about his family, employment history and especially about the Stonewall War. I have taken the newspaper information at face value.

* * *

From the Trinidad Historical Society, I received copies of the contemporary interviews of once prominent citizen of Trinidad and Las Animas County. The interview notes were the work product of the Federal Writers' Project.

Each state had a writer's project whose writings were combined into a series of state guidebooks. Between 1935 and 1943, the government created the Works Progress Administration (WPA)

The WPA employed as many as 3.8 million Americans. Some of the WPA's programs were for unemployed artists, writers and musicians. These were collectively known as "Federal One." While most of the WPA programs hired manual laborers for construction projects, "Federal One" hired to support unemployed cultural workers.

The Trinidad Historical Society's help included articles about significant criminal cases or events during Finch's' time as Las Animas Sheriff. The official sheriff's history records that in 1899 Finch got shot and killed during the apprehension of a gang of train robbers. So, for the second time, the reports of his death were greatly exaggerated.

The records sometimes provided the dates for some of Duane Finch's jobs. But other jobs, while confirmed by multiple records, do not clarify dates, or present conflicting dates. In these few instances, during his days in Trinidad and after the stage company, I have been left to choose the most believable sequence.

The story of Duane Finch's experience at Andersonville is based on the historical descriptions in the National Park Service Series website about the civil war prison camp.

The references to the Freemasons are based on my having been a Master Mason for fifty-three years. His time in a Medical Holding Company are based on my experiences and hospitalization during the Gulf War. I have honored masonic ritual secrets, while reflecting the ageless depth of masonic charity.

Redeeming Henry Wirz

When the war ended, Captain Henry Wirz, the stockade commander at Andersonville, was arrested and charged with "murder, in violation of the laws of war." Tried and convicted by a military tribunal, he was hanged in Washington, D. C. on November 10, 1865. He was the only Confederate officer charged or convicted of a war crime. Somebody needed to pay.

In fact, Capt. Wirz tried his best to create a safe environment for prisoners and to secure adequate rations. The political leadership of the Confederacy ignored or rejected each of his attempts.

Thomas Nast

Nast is best known for creating the iconic Santa Claus image, memorialized in ads by the Coca Cola Co. Nast is also considered having been the originator of 'political cartoons.' He was the principal illustrator for the Harper's Weekly Journal during the Civil War. His distinctive style and artistic skills are displayed in this book's cover image, political cartoons and many others.

Harper's Weekly: Journal of Civilization

Harper's Weekly was published from 1857 to 1916 as a political magazine based in New York City that covered news, literature, and illustrations. It was published by Harper & Brothers and was a prominent journal during the Civil War. Once the Civil War began, Harper's Weekly took a firm Unionist stance and was increasingly supportive of emancipation and black civil rights. It was widely read by soldiers in the Union army. Thomas Nast was the magazine's original illustrator and political cartoonist.

Successor magazines from the same publisher include Harper's Magazine and Harper's Bazaar.

About the Author

After returning from the Air Force, Stuart L. Scott worked as staff in a juvenile detention facility, moved on to adult probation and finally to federal probation and parole. In 1978 he returned to the military as a reserve agent with the Army CID, including work with the special Protective Service Section, guarding Cabinet officials and other dignitaries.

Born and raised in the San Francisco Bay area, he has lived with his wife in Moscow, Idaho since 1981. Believing that we only go around once in life and that one job is never enough, his other careers include: professional winemaker, college instructor, director of a school for disabled children and stained-glass artist. His introduction to commercial writing came as an outgrowth of an introduction to the therapeutic value of journaling as part of a Veterans' PTSD counseling group.

SLS@Turbonet.com

Also By This Author

The Tooth Fairy

A story as cold as a Spokane winter about what happens when a crook chooses the wrong victim.

The Grand Tetons

The Texas bank robber who carries twin 38's.

Idaho Catch and Release

Husband and wife pornographers who give a new meaning to what's really a crime.

The Deal

The 1976 case of a crooked politician revisited in 2016.

Available at Amazon in paperback and on Kindle
ISBN:9781732246812

Sample from *Gritty, Grisly, Greedy*

The Grand Tetons

It was a hot August day in 1969 when Janet Lee walked into the center of Clarksville, Texas from where she parked her car in the Seven Eleven lot by the highway. Her hometown in Oklahoma looked just like this one. The square of every small Texas town had either a courthouse or a city hall on one side. Across the square was the bank, and between the two, in the center of the square, was a flagpole with a cannon at its base. The red, white and blue of the Texas flag hung just below Old Glory. With no breeze, the two flags blended into one mass of colors.

"I wonder if this is the Clarksville that The Monkees sang about?" she muttered as she crossed the square. The Walmart that had come to town last year had already driven out many of the local merchants. The storefronts on the square were all empty except for the Farmers and Merchants Bank. That was all she needed. It was more than that. It was a gift, and you could make more of it.

Entering the bank, Janet let her eyes adjust to the interior lighting. A manager sat at a desk in the rear of the lobby. She doodled on a withdrawal slip before taking it over to the lone teller who stood at one of the three stations.

"Hello." She switched on her most dazzling smile, tossed her ash-blond hair and beamed at the young man with her bright blue eyes.

"Good morning, Ma'am." He flushed. "Ar…eh…I mean good afternoon." He finally managed to get out, "How can I help you today?"

"Well thank you." She smiled and passed the withdrawal slip across the counter. "I'd like to make a withdrawal, please."

Slowly she opened the front of her short denim jacket, first one side and then the other, to reveal the white fishnet of her tank top. The smile on the face of the young man disappeared. His eyes were drawn to the rose-pink nipples that seemed to be staring at him through the mesh. He tried looking back up to her brilliant smile but couldn't. From her round, firm breasts the rosy nipples were still staring up at his eyes. Then his gaze dropped to the large brown wood gun butt that hugged the flat of her stomach. Some emblem, a Texas star perhaps, was inset on the grip.

"Take all the money from your drawer and put it in the bag, honey." She held eye contact with him, even though his stare had not yet left the gun. She removed a white flour sack from her back pocket and passed it across the counter. "Please don't spoil either of our days by pushing any alarm. Momma needs the money for her surgery, and I'm just trying to be a good daughter."

When the full bag slid back across the counter, she spoke again. "Wait just a bit before you do anything." She did her best to portray both innocence and vulnerability by managing a small frown. Then, buttoning the middle button on her jacket, she walked out of the bank, but not out of his dreams.

* * * *

"So can you tell me what she was wearing?" asked Deputy Sheriff Muldrow, from Red River County.

"Denim jeans and a denim jacket," was the response. The answer from the teller started the deputy writing in his notebook as they sat across the table in the bank's employee lounge.

"What color was her hair?"

"I don't remember." The teller stared at the table, avoiding eye contact with the deputy.

"What about the color of her eyes?"

"I don't remember." The deputy pressed on.

"Did she have a gun?"

"Yes, there was a gun."

At last, they we're back on track. "Okay, what kind of a gun was it?"

"Big gun." He shook his head apologetically.

Trying not to let his frustration show, the deputy tried again. "Is there anything else you can recall?" The teller didn't seem to hear the question. After what seemed like a minute, Muldrow repeated the question.

"She had a beautiful smile. I just couldn't seem to tear my eyes away."

"From her smile?"

"Yes, that's right, from her smile." Then he shut up. He wasn't about to volunteer that all he could recall were her beautiful breasts.

Prisoners of War is simultaneously a love story, a mystery and a history, all woven together. Everything of a historical nature is true to the best of my knowledge and research. Conflict between love and duty. Conflict between love of country and the love of your life. How far would you go to win back your love, when the government has taken her away? Fear, racism and abiding love collide in 1942 America, when your only crime was being born Japanese.

Kirkus review says, "The author has a gift for sympathetic portrayal of antagonistic views."
and
"An affecting, historically keen story."

Available at Amazon in paperback and on Kindle
ISBN: 978-1-7322468-2-9

Sample from Prisoners of War

Chapter 1: Keyport, 1941

It was late the morning of December 7 when I heard a commotion at the Olson house next door—crying and swearing. It sounded like a family fight, loud and vulgar even, yet personal. Sounds of confusion were also coming from the main gate at the nearby Keyport, Washington, Torpedo Station. I was used to the noise in the Keyport machine shop where I worked, building torpedoes for the Bureau of Ordinance. This was a different sound. Trucks were moving, people were shouting and booted feet were running. Behind me, through his closed door, I heard my roommate Duano's voice.

"God damn it, you guys!"

He emerged half-dressed with jeans and socks on, his shirt and shoes in hand.

"Sunday morning is supposed to be quiet, Pat. What is the problem with those assholes?"

"Come on. Get dressed, and we'll head over to the gate and see what's up."

We walked out past our neighbor's store and into the street. Up ahead, one of the many Marines standing around turned briefly to respond to our shouted question.

"What the hell's going on?"

"The Japs bombed our fleet at Pearl Harbor. We're at war."

His words stopped us both in our tracks. In the confusion at the main gate, I saw a familiar figure, Captain Olson, my landlord and chief of security at Keyport.

"Captain Olson! Is there something we should do to help? Just tell us what you need."

"Thanks, McBride. For now, it would be best for you just to go home until your next shift. If I need to organize work or defense parties, I'll send someone over to get you. Bad business, this."

Then Olson turned away to direct the makeshift barricade being erected outside the gate. Still stunned, Duano and I walked back to our house and sat down on the porch to watch the action at the main gate. I stepped inside and turned on the radio, hoping for, all the while dreading, more news.

The news was on every station. The few details available were being repeated and occasionally augmented when more information came in from across the Pacific. We didn't have a phone, so I tried calling home using the pay phone at the Keyport Mercantile. Again and again, I turned the rotary dial, trying to call San Bruno. I tried my parents' house first and then my fiancée's home, but every attempt rang as a busy signal.

Walking away from the pay phone through the bright sun of this particular Sunday morning, I would never have believed that inside of two years I would become a traitor to my country.

Meet the three women who decide not to be victims anymore.

"A deceptively slim yet viciously potent slice of female retribution." Kirkus Reviews

Available at Amazon in paperback and on Kindle
ISBN: 978-1-7322468-6-7

Sample from Spirit Lake Payback

Prologue: Spokane, Washington

June 6, 1995

The Spokane newspaper article ran under the banner, **Residents Rush to Plug Leaky Lake.**

"It was only last week that this reporter's boat was in the water, but now it's beached on weeds and mud, here next to my dock. State officials aren't sure why the lake is leaking, but they know it's leaking a lot of water into the Spokane aquifer. The state believes that holes are the main problem. The spokesman for the Idaho Department of Lands explained. 'It's tough to tell legitimate holes from the occasional moose footprint, or one dug by a toad when the lakebed was dry. The trick is to stir up some muck near a suspected hole. If it gets sucked down, the hole is declared a "leaker" and resealed. Unless you see it happen, it's hard to believe.'"

June 10, 1995

Today the follow-up newspaper headline was an eye catcher. **Spirit Lake Sink Hole Collapses to Reveal Skeletal Remains.**

"Idaho authorities interrupted the efforts of local homeowners to seal the continuing plague of sink holes when an undetermined number of human skeletons were discovered in the bottom muck of a collapsed sink hole. A 250 ft. area on the south shore of the lake has been cordoned off. State and tribal archeologists are preparing to excavate the site, hoping to determine the provenance of the apparent ancient burial ground."

June 30, 1995

Spirit Lake Sink Hole Linked to Mob Body Dump.

The Kootenai County Sheriff in his lakeside press conference revealed, "Those remains appear to be 40 to 60 years old and not a tribal burial ground as we first imagined. The archeological excavation has yielded up scraps of clothing and shoes that confirm the approximate age of the remains. The Coeur d'Alene tribal Archeologist called us in yesterday when he removed a skull from the pit and noticed fillings and gold teeth. Once the site is excavated, the identification of the remains will begin. Until that time, we have a bit of a mystery on our hands."

A combined local, state and federal multi-agency task force recovered nine bodies from their Spirit Lake dump site. Skeletal remains had become disarticulated into a pile of anonymous bones, awaiting re-assembly. When they were dumped was a mystery, but bullet holes in many of the skulls and cut marks on bones all pointed to violent ends for the nine unknowns.

The last US Mail wagon robbery in the country happened in Nevada and the stolen payroll money was never found. To boost his newspaper sales, Joe Pulitzer sent staff West to cover this incident.
Treasure hunters from all across the country came seeking the goldmine payroll money, and polio came with the visitors!

Available at Amazon in paperback and on Kindle
ISBN: 978-1-7375429-1-9

Sample from Last Ghost Dance

Love and Death in a Small Town

Verrall Black sprang from the swarthy, dark *Reivers* of the Scottish Lowlands, a place of constant border warfare. His beard matched the black of his hair and eyes. He stood 5 foot 9 inches tall, wire tough, the sinews of his forearms bulging beneath their canopy of black hair. His coloration lived on in his oldest daughter, Melba. His second child, Doris, had her mother's red hair and pale skin that would too soon freckle.

The Black family came to Nevada in the 1880s. Verrall Black used the proceeds from his family's success in cattle ranching to open a store in Deeth. The sign above the porch overhang read, "Deeth Mercantile—General Merchandise." The town boasted 500 souls in 1908, and his was the only store. The local Paiute band sold pine nuts and deer hide gloves to the mercantile.

Business was good, supplying the locals from Starr Valley, miners from the gold mines at Jarbidge, and cowboys from The Union Land and Cattle Company that ran over 1,000 head of cattle on the sage-covered range surrounding the town.

Across the dirt street from the Mercantile was the Post Office. As the railhead for the Jarbidge mines, Deeth became the largest town in Northern Nevada. Jarbidge gold fueled an expanding local economy.

An opera house, roller rink, barbershop and ice cream parlor opened. Solidifying Deeth as a town was a two-cell city jail, a one-room school, a Chinese laundry and a boarding house and restaurant.

The boarding house was not to be confused with the "Women's Boarding House" that operated above the town's only tavern and dance hall, owned by John Hudson. Cowboys, miners and railroad men now had more opportunities to shed their burden of heavy gold

coins. Three "working ladies," Minnie, Mabel, and Lottie, rented the rooms upstairs. Hudson was their landlord, not their employer.

Lottie Loomis was a willowy brunette from California. She had left her home heading for Denver but only made it as far as Deeth. She had the looks, personality and discipline to do more than trade what she had for what she needed to get by; she aspired to operate a house of her own. She exuded seduction along with raw sexuality. Lottie's real talent was effortlessly convincing men that she wanted them as much as they wanted her. She flirted. She teased. She told every man that found his way into her arms, "You are different from all the men I've known before." Unfortunately, John Hudson believed her.

The saloon owner had set his sights on Lottie. He dreamed about her constantly, in fantasies both erotic and domestic. He took every opportunity to keep her in his sight. Lacking self-esteem, he never risked the rejection, or worse, ridicule by showing his feelings.

John had a hired bartender in the evening, allowing him to float between being a greeter and piano player. As he played his piano below, his mind couldn't escape the thought of Lottie in bed with another man just above him. One Saturday night, he watched Lottie ascend the stairs with a customer, laughing and smiling at the man. His control cracked. His eyes leaked tears as he played the ivory keys. Onward his imagination led him. She was up there now, right above his head, sharing her charms with someone who didn't love her or deserve her as he did.

His hands balled into fist and the fists crashed onto the keyboard. The clang of the keys rang out over the conversations from the barroom and dance floor. As the music stopped, so did the dancers and the talk. The room went silent when John drew out a Colt revolver from his inside coat pocket and began shooting into the dance hall ceiling. "Boom-boom-boom."

No one moved. One group of four men immediately turned their table sideways for a barricade. Ben Kuhl, a small-time thief, had just introduced his two friends, Bob McGinty and Ed Beck, to Fred Searcy, a local teamster. Kuhl believed Fred, who drove a freight wagon, might be a good man to know. He'd file away Searcy's name and his job for possible later use.

The four looked over the tabletop. Every eye in the room was now focused on Hudson. Adjusting his aim, he let loose again, "boom-boom-boom," emptying his gun into the pale plaster ceiling. The crowd watched as he turned away from the piano and dropped the pistol onto the floorboards at his feet. His elbows went to his knees as he wept into his hands. Drops of smelly liquid began to fall through the bullet holes and drip onto his shirt.

Ed Smiley, the bartender, finally judged it safe to approach his sobbing boss. He picked up the gun, passing it to Dennis McDermott. Ed then walked through the cloud of black powder smoke and climbed the stairs from the dance hall to the bedrooms. From the hallway, the two other doors were cracked open. Other upstairs customers, half-clad, peeked out. The door to Lottie's room was still shut. Ed paused at the door, listening. Finally, he spoke the first words since the shooting. "I'm coming in."

No one was alive inside the small room. Two naked figures lay entangled on the metal-framed bed. Lottie's body lay face down astride her male guest. Blood pooled on the bedding and the floor from two bullet wounds to her upper body. Her companion was shot in the thigh. Other wound tracks, concealed by their bodies, were dripping blood onto the floor. There it mixed with the liquid contents of a chamber pot under the bed, also shot through. The ammonia from urine mixed with the iron smell of their blood.

Ed backed up, closed the door and walked down the stairs to the dance hall.

Hudson was still seated on his piano stool, head in hands. Word had spread out from the bar to the de facto leaders of the town. Verrall Black, Ben Armstrong and Bob Anderson clustered together with Dennis McDermott in the center of the room.

Ed took two steps toward the men before speaking. "Lottie and Roy Wooden, the section foreman, are both dead." Standing aside as the four men whispered among themselves, Smiley posed the unspoken question on many minds. "What's to be done now?"

Verrall Black spoke for the group. "We've been talking it over. Ben and Bob will take Hudson over to the jail for the night. We'll ask Mabel and Minnie to clean up Lottie's body and wind her tight in a sheet. You and I will do the same for Roy."

"Then what?" asked Ed.

"You get some help, maybe the other men upstairs, and move the two bodies to the cattle company shed for now. That will keep them cold and safe until somebody comes up from Elko."

Smiley nodded his agreement. The five men separated to deal with their appointed tasks. Hudson's shirt was soaked by the drops falling from above. Fate had pissed on him again.

As they separated, one of the group turned and stopped the bartender with a question." Did she know how he felt?"

"I guess not."

Later Saturday night, Verrall and Ed Smiley took two blankets, a plate of biscuits and stew, hard candy and a cup of hot coffee over to John Hudson. They had no concerns about Hudson trying to escape.

"John, these should help you through the night. There's a slop bucket under the bunk. You may have already found that."

Hudson nodded that he had. He sat on the wooden bunk, staring at the cement floor, but neither spoke nor made eye contact with Black.

Verrall nudged Hudson with the plate and offered the hot cup of coffee. Hudson took both as Ed Smiley entered the cell and placed the blankets on the bunk.

As the cell door closed, Hudson looked up and gave a momentary smile. "Thank you." After a long pause, he spoke again. "They're dead, aren't they." It was not a question.

Ed Smiley delivered the answer as the cell door closed. "Yes. Both."

In the morning, John Hudson was dead by his own hand, hung with an improvised noose fashioned from strips of blankets braided together and attached to bars in the cell window. His meager last meal lay untouched on the bunk.

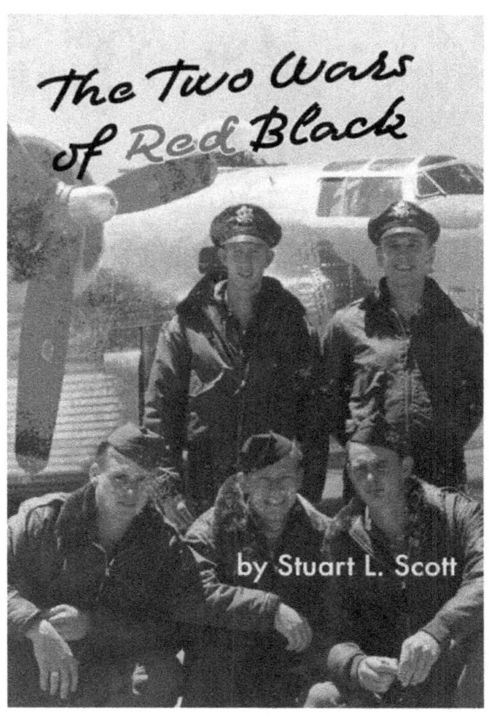

The wartime adventures of William "Red" Black, with just enough
fiction to connect the true events.
He went from a childhood on a chicken farm in Stockton, California to
navigating a B-24 over Europe. Shot down over Germany, he escaped to
Sweden.
He stayed in the service after WWII.
"Lieutenant Black, what would you like to do, now?"
"Not being able to shoot back is bullshit.
I want to be a fighter pilot!"
He flew an F-82 Twin Mustang night fighter
in the Korean War.
Discover the untold costs of war on a man who chose to defend us all.

Available at Amazon in paperback and on Kindle
ISBN 978-1-7375429-1-9